MAYAN STRAWBERRIES

THE JOSEPH RADKIN SERIES

Book 1

Strange Inheritance

Book 2

The Genesis Files

Book 3

Judgement of Death

Book 4

Paper Cuts

Book 5

Mayan Strawberries

Joseph Radkin Investigations

BOOK 5

MAYAN STRAWBERRIES

BOB BIDERMAN

BLACK
APOLLO
PRESS

First published in Great Britain by Black Apollo Press' 2012

ISBN: 9781900355407

For information about our other titles, please go to our website: www.blackapollo.com

Before the world was created, Calm and Silence were the great kings that ruled. Nothing existed, there was nothing. Things had not yet been drawn together, the face of the earth was unseen. There was only motionless sea, and a great emptiness of sky. There were no men anywhere, or animals. No birds or fish, no crabs. Trees, stones, caves, grass, forests – none of these existed yet. There was nothing that could roar or run. Nothing that could tremble or cry in the air. Flatness and emptiness, only the sea, alone and breathless. It was night; Silence stood in the dark.

From: Popul Vuh – The Great Mythological Book of the Ancient Maya.

Chapter 1

THE SHRILLNESS OF the ring jangled his subconscious like a silicon Siren calling to a timewarped Odysseus. He opened his eyes and looked up from the couch. The room was a blur. Everything seemed off kilter as if the foundation had slipped during the night bending the perpendicular. For a moment he wondered where he was. Then he remembered and wondered where she was.

The phone rang again and he reached for it with a grunt. "Polly?" he called down the line. He waited for a response but the only thing he heard was a hollow roar, like an ocean in a sea shell. The sound of emptiness.

Maybe it was all in his head. Tympanic feedback, after all, was one sign of ageing. He was about to hang up when he heard a voice. It was a woman's voice, but not the one he wanted.

"Joseph? Joseph Radkin?"

"Yeah. Who's this?" he said with annoyance.

"Elizabeth Manning..."

The voice came from the blue like a born again memory searching out its maker.

"Joseph? You do still remember, don't you?"

"Sure I remember."

"I'm sorry we've been out of touch so long. So much has happened..."

"To everyone...everywhere."

"How are you? Are you still at the paper?" Her voice sounded like she already knew.

"No. I left soon after you and Felix. You're still together, I assume."

"Still together." There was a slight hesitation. "We're living in Ecstasy now."

"I thought you always were..."

"No. Not the emotion. The town...."

"You mean that farming place up north? What the hell are you doing up there? Milking cows?"

"Running the local newspaper."

He heard himself chuckle. But it was like coughing with broken ribs it hurt. To ease the pain, he lit up a cigarette. "Come on!", he said. "Pull the other one!" He took a drag on his smoke and let the narcotic effect take over as he thought back to the days when Felix and Elizabeth were the Dick Powel and Myrna Loy of the metropolitan newspaper set complete with wirehaired terrier. Back then, before the coke-heads ruled the roost, they had been the epitome of three martini glamor.

"It's true," she said. "We've been there over a year already."

He watched the coils of smoke from his cigarette evaporate in the air and thought that in a world stood on its head nothing much surprised him anymore. "Must be great for six months or so," he said, bringing the phone over to the couch and letting his body drop into the cushions. "But after that, what do you find to write about? How many stories can you do on the sex life of the potato?"

"Actually, it's strawberry country..."

"Strawberries ... sorry."

"It's very beautiful up there. Really." She didn't sound like she was in ecstasy.

"You OK?" he asked.

"No. That's why I wanted to talk with you..."

"After all these years? Why me?"

"I couldn't think of anyone else..."

"Isn't there a village priest or something?" He took another drag on his cigarette and let the smoke curl from his mouth. "How about Felix?"

"It's Felix I wanted to talk about."

"Concerning what?"

8

She hesitated a moment. "It has something to do with a murder..."

"Felix?" His voice carried a note of extreme doubt.

"Felix and I have been covering a story about a murder case that happened up there a while ago. About a farm laborer who got stabbed in the strawberry fields..."

He stared at the receiver as if it were the middle of the night and someone had just rung up to say that a man had gotten mugged in the park. It was hard to get his juices flowing for something that had become such an everyday occurrence. In the city a simple act of violence had about as much journalistic appeal as a cat puking up a mouse.

"I know little murders aren't big news in San Francisco, but they are in Ecstasy," she went on. "And, really, there's more to it ..."

"There's always more to it, Elizabeth. You know that. The problem is where it takes you."

"I hope it takes you to Zuni's," she said. "I'll only be in the city another hour or so and I'd like a chance to talk..."

Chapter 2

IF SOMEONE HAD asked him why he went, he couldn't have given them a straight answer. Not that he always felt the need to give straight answers, but this time he couldn't if he wanted.

Maybe it had to do with feeling claustrophobic in the house, he thought as he parked the car around the corner from Zuni's. Or maybe he remembered the scent of her perfume. But one thing was for certain, it had nothing to do with the death of a farm worker in a small California town. And if her object was to get him involved, he hadn't the slightest intention.

Of course, he often felt that way in the beginning. But

this had all the makings of nothing times ten. It was the bleeding heart syndrome in spades, he thought. Everyone had a story that tugged at their emotions. Put under a magnifying glass and written with creative adjectives, a housefly with torn wings could be made to seem like Camille. He'd done it himself when he was starving for work. But, in a cynical world, where the unimaginable was becoming more and more commonplace, few stories amounted to anything significant – really significant, that is. After all, how much blood could you dredge up before it started to seem like water? How much death before bodies became like so many carcasses hanging stiffly on a hook? How much fraud and malfeasance before it looked as if the entire world was on the take and it just didn't matter anymore?

He was thinking of all this as he rounded the corner. Then suddenly another reason dawned on him why he had consented to come. Zuni's was the new place where all the trendy people went to be seen. And, perhaps out of journalistic curiosity, he had a vague sense of wanting to know what was in fashion and why – if fashion had a reason, that is.

Joseph wasn't much into trendy hangouts. The Adler Museum Cafe in North Beach was more his style with its booze, jazz and funk. But Zuni's was different, he had to admit. It was as if someone had taken a bit of the Mojave Desert and shipped it to Frisco lock, stock and cactus and then hired an Indian to reconstitute it as a restaurant. The surprising thing was, in appearance it made a damn fine oasis. But that was before he caught a look at the prices.

Even though it was off hours, the place was sizzling like only a hot spot that's still on the cooker could. Once inside, he realized that in order to find a seat you probably had to have a recognizable face or else wait a few months for the fire to cool down. He didn't have the face nor was he willing to wait till the flames were doused.

He didn't have to. The head waiter approached and

looked him up and down. But instead of telling him to get lost, he said, "A lady back there claims to know you, sir."

He couldn't have missed her. Nobody could. She was wearing more dangling turquoise than Zuni's should have allowed, unless they wanted their customers to compete with the decorations. On the other hand, she probably would have competed anyway with her raving mane of bright red hair. When she stood up every head seemed to pop out of joint staring at her.

Trying to be cool, he causally sauntered over to her table, aware that all eyes were shifted on him. And those were powerful eyes, he figured. Eyes he might have come up against in former investigations probably having to do with fraudulent stock manipulations. Now he was the focus of their probing stares, he thought, as his stomach turned sour.

"Joseph!" She stood up, sparkling with flashes of refracted light from all her polished bangles. "It's so nice to see you again!" She gave him a peck on the cheek. "What are you having to drink?" she asked as he thankfully manoeuvered into the chair she had reserved for him.

"Maybe a bicarbonate," he said.

Her eyes were still a glittering emerald green specked with tiny flakes of orange, he noticed as she motioned to the waiter and ordered a bottle of mineral water. He had always wondered whether that color existed in real life or was a creation of the contact lens industry. But, whatever its origin, it was very effective in offsetting all that turquoise, he decided.

She smiled and he felt that special radiance she could so effortlessly project. Some people have it, he thought, a soft magnetic field that draws things into their orbit like a tune played on a magic flute. Depending on the tune, you could either end up happily on Corfu or else shipwrecked on a desert island.

"Catch me up on the last ten years," she said, reaching out across the table and touching his hand.

"Marriage, two kids, some interesting stories, lots of

11

boring ones, problems with money, problems with editors ... and a growing sense of malaise and discontent." He poured himself a glass of fizzy water from the bottle the waiter had just left and said "How about you?"

"It's as if I entered a different universe," she replied. She said it as if the statement explained itself.

"You mean Ecstasy isn't?" he said, half mocking, half wondering what she meant.

She shook her head and the glow seemed to melt. "When Felix was asked to resign, I was ready to leave San Francisco anyway. I was sick of the daily grind. We didn't really know what we wanted to do. Felix, of course, wasn't worried in the least. He always seems to land on his feet, doesn't he?"

Joseph nodded. He knew only too well.

"Anyway, I was all in a dither. I wanted to get away, but I needed something to do. Then – well you know how opportunity just seems to fall into your lap sometimes..."

"I've heard about things like that happening to people forced to grow up with a mouth full of silver spoons..."

"It can happen to anyone, Joseph," she said. "You don't question things like that. It happened and it was as if fate held out her hand and said, 'Here it is! Take it!' And there it was. A little newspaper office of our very own in a small town a million miles away from anywhere. A little Eden of fertile land and clear blue skies. A town where people smiled at you and said hello when you passed them on the street..."

Joseph felt his stomach ache worse than before. He emptied his glass of seltzer and poured himself another one. "Is that what Felix was looking for, too?" he said with a trace of disbelief in his voice.

"I thought so at the time," she said. Her eyes no longer seemed focused on him but had taken on a dreamy look. "Anyway, for a while it was marvellous. We built our house and set up the newspaper just a broadsheet, really. We brought it out occasionally, whenever we felt like. No real deadlines. No hassles. Our only problem was learning to set type and figuring out how to proof it without a mirror."

"Sort of a twentieth century newspaper version of Little House on the Prairie, I guess?" he said, barely able to hide his sarcasm.

"It might have started out that way," she said, fingering a bracelet of silver and jade. "But it evolved very quickly. We started taking it more seriously. There's something enormously cathartic about going back to the basics of journalism I mean actually getting ink on your hands ..."

He looked at her hands, so silky white, and could hardly imagine them stained with ink.

"We found ourselves suddenly tapping into the lifeblood of a community in a way we never, ever, were able to do here..."

He noticed there were lines at the corners of her eyes – lines he hadn't seen before. He found himself wondering how age had affected her.

"It was both extremely beautiful and very frightening..." she continued.

"Frightening? How so?" he asked.

She had a pensive look; her face was calm but there was also something curious about her expression something he couldn't define. "There are so many layers to life, aren't there, Joseph? When you scratch one, you expose another. If you dig under that, another one appears. And soon you start to realize that it never ends."

"I always found the layers end pretty fast, myself," he said, "once you get to the bedrock which usually consists of greed, lust or fear. Sometimes all three. Occasionally you might hit integrity, but there's no story in that is there? At least that's what the publishers say." He fixed his eyes on her face, trying to figure out what she really wanted to tell him. "What about the murder?" he asked.

Reaching for her bag, which had been conspicuously placed next to her glass, she opened it and pulled out a photograph which she handed to him. It was a picture of a young man, no older than twenty he figured. He had a sunburnt face, with high cheek bones and jet black hair. It was a face that wouldn't have looked out of place in a migrant labor camp. But, at the same time, it was different. He couldn't' put his finger on what the difference was, exactly. Maybe it was the look of boyish wonder.

"His name is Salvador Garcia," she said, fixing her eyes on him. "He's been in prison for the last three years serving a life sentence."

"Too bad. He looks like a nice kid," Joseph said, handing the photo back to her.

"The problem is that he's innocent." Her eyes studied his face for a reaction.

"Lot's of people are, Elizabeth," he said. "The prisons are full of them. Would you like me to apologize for the system? Or maybe you'd like to."

"No," she said, without a blink, "I wouldn't like to apologize. I'd like you to listen to what I have to say without feeling obliged to be sarcastic."

"I wasn't being sarcastic," he replied, "I was being honest." But even through his rawness he realized that for her this clearly was a moving subject. "Go on," he continued, as he poured himself the last of the fizzy water. "I'm listening."

"A few months ago we met a woman who lives outside of town. She told us she was a juror in a murder trial some years back and for all those years she was obsessed with the fear that she had convicted an innocent man ..."

"That's a pretty common feeling, Elizabeth," he said. "Any juror of conscience finds themselves racked with doubt for a long time after they send someone to prison. If you're a sensitive person, you're bound to feel that way even if there was overwhelming evidence for conviction."

"I know that, Joseph," she replied. "It was the rest of what she had to say that got us interested. You see, the young man in question wasn't an ordinary farm worker – not your typical Mexican bracerro, that is. He's a Central American

14

Indian. It seems that for years now Indian refugees from El Salvador and Guatemala have been streaming over the border into Mexico. Some of them have managed to link up with the migrant labor force, the fruit and vegetable pickers who follow the harvest. Most of these refugees, however, don't have proper documentation – they either travel with forged papers or else sneak across the Rio Grande into the US and hire themselves out to unscrupulous farm labor agents who pay them a pittance if they pay them at all..."

"And many of them are angry and hostile," Joseph cut in. "For good reason, of course. Unfortunately, sometimes they drink and get into fights..."

"Yes, that's true. And, also, unfortunately, sometimes the wrong person gets arrested when the police come to sort out the mess. A town like Ecstasy, so far north, doesn't have many Spanish speaking residents. In fact, one farm worker tends to look very much like another at least to the people up there."

"Maybe you could get to the point," said Joseph, not even trying to hide his exasperation. "If you're saying that some people, especially if they don't have money for a decent lawyer, are caught in the net because the cops and the courts need convictions and don't have the patience to follow the niceties of law even to the point of giving a pig's snout if they snag the right man, I believe you." His face took on a tired expression as he continued: "And you know what? Even with all the insanity, once in a while, maybe even fifty percent of the time, they manage to get someone who deserves to be sent away. Sometimes people actually do commit crimes, Elizabeth even Central American Indian boys with pretty faces!"

She was gazing at him, unblinking; her green eyes were void of anger. There was only sadness in them at least that's all he saw. Maybe he had overstepped the bounds, he thought.

He rubbed the side of his face and looked down at his empty glass. "Forget it, Elizabeth," he said. "I'm in a bit of a mess. Polly took the kids and walked out on me the other day."

"I'm sorry to hear that, Joseph," she said, reaching out and touching his hand again. "Do you want to tell me about it?"

"She just got tired of me feeling sorry for myself, I guess ... and drowning myself in liquor." His lips had worked themselves into a tiny, contorted grin. "But she'll be back. It isn't the first time and it probably won't be the last."

"Poor, sweet Joseph," she said, trying to look sympathetic.

"Poor, maybe. Sweet, never," he replied, angry he exposed himself like that. As a diversion from his embarrassment, he narrowed his eyes and said, "How does Felix fit into all of this?"

"I told you, we were both involved in this story ..."

He shook his head. "When you phoned, you told me that you wanted to talk about Felix and that it had something to do with a murder."

"The story is far more complex than the simple murder of a farm worker, Joseph. We realized that soon after we began looking into it..."

"How so?" he asked, fixing his gaze on a soft twitch that had started under one of her amazing green eyes.

"I'm not sure. All I know is that once we started asking questions about the murder, the attitude of people quickly changed. It was like probing molluscs – at the slightest touch, the shell snaps shut. But it was more than that. Strange things started happening. We suddenly found ourselves very isolated in the community..."

"That's not surprising, is it?" Joseph said. "I mean, you've been there for a while, but you're still relative strangers. It probably would take you ten years before you really gained their trust. And here you are hanging out their dirty laundry for them..."

She took a little mirror from her purse and inspected her face. Then she brought out a frilly handkerchief and brushed something from the corner of her eye. When she put the mirror back, her expression had changed. He thought it was like putting on an invisible mask.

"I am worried about Felix," she said. "And it does have to do with the murder story. A few weeks ago, he began receiving some curious phone calls – curious in that after he had finished talking with whoever called, he became very preoccupied and uncommunicative ..."

"How do you know the phone calls had anything to do with the story the two of you were working on?" His eyes were still fixed on her face. It was one of the few things he had learned from the cops. A face was a map and if you knew where you wanted to go you could chart your course through its myriad of expressions. Cops, however, were notoriously bad navigators. But they had the right idea.

"Because I happened to pick up the extension. I heard someone making threatening remarks..."

"Was it a voice you knew?" he asked.

She shook her head. "I couldn't say for certain."

"Did you tell the police?"

"There's only one policeman in town," she said. "And I really wouldn't trust him."

He shook his head. "That doesn't sound good, Elizabeth. Maybe you should think about selling your house and moving back to a place where cops are corrupt but at least there's more than one of them ..."

"It's our home," she said. Her expression was stubborn and it made her look even more beautiful to him.

"Have you spoken to Felix about this? What does he say?"

"Felix has become very taciturn," she replied with a sigh. "When he gets like that, there's really no talking to him."

"But he must have said something!" Joseph demanded impatiently.

"Only that he'd take care of it."

He pursed his lips, like a doctor about to diagnose cancer. "It's a rule of thumb in journalism that art historians should stick to the museum beat. If I wandered through an antiquities collection, I'd probably end up smashing a few vases. On

17

the other hand, I wouldn't be dumb enough to go messing around with a nest of hornets in my own backyard unless I felt pretty damn sure about what I was doing. They have a nasty habit of taking their revenge in the most vulnerable places."

"That's why I've come to you for advice," she said with a little smile. "You've had experience with things like this and..."

"And what?" he said, narrowing his eyes.

"And you're someone I can trust."

He wished he could say the same about her. But he couldn't.

She looked at him and smiled even more sweetly. "Joseph, I'd like it if you could come up to Ecstasy and spend the weekend with us."

"I'm sorry," he said, shaking his head. "I'd like to but I can't..."

Moving her body softly, almost imperceptibly, so her face came closer to his, she whispered, "Joseph, I wouldn't ask if I weren't so frightened. Please don't make me beg. I really need you..."

He took a deep whiff of her perfume and remembered the fragrance well. He closed his eyes. "OK," he muttered, regretting it even then.

When he opened his eyes again, her face was beaming. She had taken out an envelope from her purse and had laid it on the table. "Here's a map and directions how to get there. It's not hard to find." She stood up. The glow was back. "I'm sorry I have to rush. I'll expect you tomorrow for dinner. We'll have lots of time to catch up on everything then!"

She walked over to his side of the table, leaned down and brushed his cheek with her lips. "It's so good to see you again, Joseph!" she whispered.

And then she left.

He stayed seated after she had gone. He motioned to the waiter and ordered a whiskey with a beer chaser.

Chapter 3

IT WAS ABOUT a three hour drive from San Francisco up to Trinity County if you didn't stop to pick the flowers and risk a week of misery from the effects of poison oak.

The ride north along the California coast was spectacular but painfully slow. Testing the road-hugging capabilities of his 1958 MG on figure-eight curves had, long ago, ceased to be fun. So he took the direct route further east, up the super-highway, which could zip you straight to Seattle in time for the last lift to the top of the Space Needle if your car was in good shape and you left the house before the paper boy had time to throw the morning rag into the neighbor's bird bath. His car was in lousy shape; but, fortunately, he wasn't going to Seattle – not even close.

Ecstasy was a small town located in a peaceful valley of redwood and pine. It was set right below the Siskiyou Mountains near where the wild Klamath River split into the tamer Trinity and South Fork – about forty miles west of Whiskeytown and Shasta National Forest. To get there you had to turn off the freeway at Redding and head toward Eureka. On the way you passed through twenty little pitstop towns, each struggling to stay alive, with their tacky main street bars, burger joints and gasoline hangouts.

But Ecstasy was different. It had a look of affluence, at least compared to its downbeat neighbors. It was clean and green and had a rushing stream of clear blue water that ran along the outskirts, just hidden from view by a majestic row of ancient redwoods that stood like giant soldiers guarding the gates of Paradise Found.

It was twilight when he reached the bypass which led from the main road to the gently slopping hills dotted with peeka-boo dwellings, each scantily visible through a veil of bucolic opulence. They looked out over an idyllic rural setting which denizens of the concrete urban landscape sometimes dream about when the winter solstice is upon them and everything looks bleak and foul, like the frozen droppings of pigeons on the cardboard container of a homeless drunk.

The map Elizabeth had made for him was easy to follow. It led to the top of a place called Miller's Hill and then along a small road. As he drove, he saw that everything wasn't quite as prim and proper as it seemed from the distance. Up here, many of the houses were just simple cottages with cords of fuel wood piled up in front and vegetable patches in the back. In fact, further down the road it soon took on the appearance of a shanty town.

He continued on a couple of miles till the road ended abruptly at a wire fence. Joseph braked to a halt, turned off the engine of the old MG and got out.

On one side of the road was a termite ravaged wooden building that seemed to be a general store – the sign only read "Harvey's"; it didn't say what Harvey used it for. Across the street was another, larger building, its timbers as rotten as its neighbor's, but this one was clearly identified as the meeting house of the local Grange. Both buildings seemed to be deserted. Joseph glanced down at his watch. It was seven o'clock.

He strolled, casually, over to the Grange meeting hall and decided that with the addition of a cross it could easily have been a village church. The grass in the surrounding yard was high and brittle, like overbaked hay that had been left to nature. To the west, over the jagged ridge of coastal mountains, the horizon had turned a fiery red – the color of Elizabeth's hair, he thought – melting the sky above into a dusky, auburn hue. He reached for a cigarette and lit up.

Taking out the map and directions from his shirt pocket, he glanced over them again. "Miller's Road ends by the old Grange house," she had written. "There's a gate to a private road – just a piece of symbolism, actually, since it's never locked. It exists to keep the livestock in check except there's

20

no livestock anymore. However, you are required to shut it again when you've passed through. Don't ask me what for ..."

"Not any longer," he said to himself, as he glanced at the fence. The gate had been severed from its hinge. In fact, half the surrounding fence had been knocked over.

"...our house is about half a mile down the dirt road, on the other side of the pine grove. You can't miss it. Dinner will be ready at seven."

He made a face realizing again that the note had been written prior to their meeting at Zuni's. "So damn sure of herself!" he muttered as he walked back to the car.

Starting up the MG, he drove over to the entrance of the dirt road, now a good ten feet wider than it had been when the fence and gate were in tact. He noticed that there were deep markings in the ground, as if the path had been used by some heavy equipment.

He drove along the pitted surface, toward the thick grove of trees that lay ahead, and wondered how anyone got any-where up there when it rained unless they were being towed by a tractor.

Before him, the air was growing hazy, as if someone was driving in front and churning up dust. But the haze was al-most motionless; it just hovered, like a floating veil of sludge.

As he drove through the woods, he noticed the haze had grown more dense and the windows of his car had acquired a thin crust of ashlike substance. Even in the middle of the tiny forest, the sweet fragrance of pine, something he loved, was noticeably absent. Instead there was a different sort of pungence.

He thought, at first, the Mannings might have made a barbecue. But then he realized that he was still too far away, unless the barbecue was in the woods and they had burnt down half the forest. Besides, there wasn't any smoke, just a lingering, blackish smog along with a low, metallic, whining sound and a jarring, noxious odor.

It wasn't until he reached the other side of the pine grove, however, that he saw it. Once out of the woods, the road gave way to a vast, empty field. At the far, northwestern end, there was the charred remains of what had probably been a large and magnificent, house. The sound was coming from a caterpillar tractor which was plowing up the cinders.

Whatever happened had been devastating. Hardly anything remained standing, except the skeletal exterior. The rest was a carbonized mass. It was as if a fiery meteor had fallen from the sky and had vaporized everything at its point of impact.

He drove up between the remaining fire truck and a police car, set the hand brake and got out. There was a trench that had been dug around the periphery of the fire probably to contain the embers. A tall, lanky cop had finished tying up a wide, plastic ribbon around the posts which staked out the perimeter on the far side of the trench. The cop looked over at Joseph as he got out of his car and frowned.

"You got business here, bud?" the cop called out.

Gazing, numbly, at the devastation, Joseph seemed oblivious to everything but a festering mixture of guilt and abhorrence. Guilt for having been annoyed at coming. Abhorrence at what he saw.

The cop strode over to where Joseph was standing, his long legs moving over the charred grass like giant scythes.

"You got business here?" he repeated.

Joseph looked over at the wiry man who had taken off his cap and was brushing a forearm across his sweaty brow. "I was supposed to have dinner with them ..." The words seemed to fall out of his mouth on their own. He knew it was dumb when he said it.

"Dinner's off," said the cop.

Staring at his face, Joseph thought it was chiselled by a bad sculptor. His eyes had that cheap look of glass imitations used in wax museums. "Do you know what happened to the Mannings?" he asked.

Ignoring him, the cop turned sharply and called out to a

man sitting in the fire truck. "I'm going back to the station, Frank. Why don't you stop by the office on your way out? I need to talk to you about writin' up the report on this shitass mess."

"Say, can't it wait till tomorrow?" the man in the fire truck said, hoarsely. "I been here since three in the fuckin' mornin'. I got to get some shuteye, Russ!"

"OK," said the cop, getting into the police car and starting it up. "Go on home." He gunned the engine and jerked it into gear. The car shot backwards. "See you in the morning, you lazy sonofabitch!" he called out, gesturing from the window with his long, bony arm. He turned the wheel so the car spun in the direction of the pine grove, threw the car into forward and took off in a cloud of dust.

Joseph walked over to the fire truck. "You know what happened to the folks who lived here?" he asked, calling up to the man inside who was scribbling something on a pad of green paper.

The man's face was a thick, spongy mass the face of someone who probably ate spoonfuls of lard for afternoon snacks. He looked down at Joseph and said, "Friends of yours?"

Joseph nodded his head. "Yeah..."

The spongyfaced man, sitting barechested in the cab of his truck , shrugged his hairy shoulders. "Don't rightly know if it were them. Don't want to jump to no conclusions. Get into trouble for that ..."

"You mean there were people trapped in there?" Joseph asked. He looked over at the devastation. "You found bodies?"

"Bodies?" The man let out a wheezelike laugh. "That fire was the hottest one I seen hereabouts. Hot enough to melt anyone inside there, I reckon..."

"Then how do you know?" Joseph looked up at him again.

"You ever smelled burning flesh? You'd known if you had. Some people say it smells like roast pork but sweeter. To me it's got a smell all its own. It's an ugly smell, but not as bad as burning dog. And that ain't as bad as burning cat."

23

"But did you find anything?" Joseph asked, feeling sick to his stomach.

"Found some bones. Two skeletons. One's woman. One's man. You can tell the sex by the pelvis. That's the only thing you got to go on. Everything else turned to gas." Then, starting up the engine of the truck, he shouted to the man on the tractor. "OK, Hank! Let's head on back!"

The man riding the caterpillar signalled by touching the tip of his cap.

"Did you know the Mannings?" Joseph yelled over the rumbling idle of the engine. "Felix and Elizabeth?"

The fireman stuck his head out the window of the cab. "Can't say that I did. But maybe you should ask the little chickadee over there. She's been watchin' like she knew somethin' about someone," he said, gesturing with his thumb.

Joseph looked over in the direction the fireman had pointed. He hadn't noticed her before – the young woman sitting on a rock underneath a shade tree, her bicycle propped against the side. She was staring out at the ruins, her head resting in the palm of her hand.

As the firetruck pulled away with the caterpillar tractor in tow, Joseph walked over to where she was sitting.

She was young early – twenties, he guessed – and fashionably slim. A widebrimmed straw hat was pulled, obliquely, over her short black hair. She was wearing a winsome black dress and kneehigh boots, which made her look both chic and frail. Her lipstick had been put on carefully, except for one smudge on the left side of her mouth which made her face into a frown. If it wasn't for the smudge, he would have wondered if she were real. But even in his confusion he did wonder what she was doing in a tiny farming town like this. Not milking the cows, he suspected.

"When did it happen?" he asked, when he got close enough for her to hear him.

"Last night, about one in the morning," she replied, without looking. "It's only a few hours ago that the other fire engines left. They brought them in from all over the county. But the place was already burnt down by the time they got here. They had to wait for it to cool before they could look for the bodies. They found what was left of Elizabeth..."

Joseph stared at her in disbelief. "How do you know it was her?"

"One of them still wore a wedding ring. It was made out of turquoise. I'd never seen another one like it. Had you, Mr. Radkin?"

He shook his head. If he hadn't felt he was lost in some mind-boggling nightmare, he would have been astounded that she knew his name. As it was, he could hardly summon up the words to ask her: "Do I know you?"

"No. But Elizabeth said you were coming for dinner. She had invited me as well..." Her face was blank, expressionless except for the painted frown. It wasn't until she turned and looked at him directly, so their eyes met, that he realized she was probably in a state of shock like him.

Pulling out his pack of cigarettes, he thumped it on the back of his hand till one of the smokes stuck out further than the rest. He held out the pack to her. She shook her head.

"Who are you!" he asked, taking one from the pack and lighting up.

"Gabriella," she said. "Gabriella Luna. I was working on the newspaper with them..."

"She never said anything about you," he muttered. But, thinking back to their meeting, she hadn't said much.

"I've only been here for a month," she replied. "Perhaps she had forgotten to say..."

He noticed a tear welling from one of her eyes. It was the only sign of emotion. He held out his pack again. This time she took one. He lit her up and watched as she drew in the vapors.

"Can we go someplace and talk?" he asked her.

The tear rolled down her cheek and dropped to the ground. Her voice was soft but definite. "Follow me back to the office," she said.

Chapter 4

THE OFFICE OF the Trinity County Gazette was on the corner of Second Street and Avenue B. It was a small, wooden house painted a sunburst yellow surrounded by a white-washed picket fence. There were tulips blooming in the front garden and bluebells waving sprightly from a window planter box. It had an almost obscene feel of life, he thought; so out of keeping with such a morbid death.

He had followed her there in the car, driving slowly behind her bicycle as she coasted the half mile or so down Miller's Hill to the center of town. Parking his car in front of the house, he got out and met her at the door. She was unlocking it as he arrived and quietly ushered him in.

The entrance led into a small reception area with a couple of antique armchairs, a couch and a redwood burl coffee table on which were strewn some artsy magazines. The room, itself, was divided in half by a low wooden partition. On the other side of the partition was a desk, with an old-fashion telephone and an upright typewriter which might have been used by old Horace Grealy himself. There was an oak side table which supported a display of cracked pottery. Next to that were several filing cabinets which appeared to be mahogany. If so, it was a waste of precious wood as they were open and seemed quite empty.

Joseph seated himself in one of the armchairs and put his hands over his eyes, trying to ease the throbbing in his head. When he looked up, she had vanished.

Glancing around, he decided the inside of the place looked more like a museum than a newspaper office with so many of Felix's artefacts hanging on the walls. He picked up one of the magazines lying on the table. It was a copy of Archaeology Today. He flipped through the pages and tossed it down again.

Suddenly, she appeared through a door at the far end of the room wearing an oversized sweater, carrying a bottle of whisky and a shot glass. She looked like maybe she had a quick one herself before coming back in.

Setting the glass on the table, she filled it to the brim, placed the bottle beside it and then sat down in a chair opposite him.

Joseph took the whisky glass, bolted down the drink and then poured himself another as she watched.

"Are you going to have one yourself or do you get your kicks looking?" he asked.

"Later," she said, still staring at him.

Meeting her gaze with a hardboiled look, he said, "You know what I've been thinking?"

She shrugged.

"A woman I knew in another life calls me up out of the blue and tells me some cockamamie story about a farm worker who gets stabbed in the fields and shows me the picture of an Indian boy who she says probably didn't do it. She says she and her prodigal husband are investigating the murder which happened a few years ago and moans about having ruffled a few feathers. She tells me this and then tells me she's frightened because somebody seems to be putting the screws on her old man. Then she leaves without paying the bill, I might add after suckering me into making a halfday's drive into hay fever country just because..." He left off to bolt down another drink.

"Just because what?" she said. "Because she needed help and trusted you?" She took a packet of tiny cigars out of a zippered pocket in the sleeve of her pullover and began unwrapping the cellophane from it.

He narrowed his eyes. "Who are you?" he asked.

"I told you my name," she said, lighting up and blowing the smoke in his direction. "Gabriella Luna."

"I'm not asking your name. I'm asking who you are – as

in what the hell you're doing here."

"I told you that, too," she said, the muscles of her young face tightening. "I work for them – worked, that is..."

"You answered an advert in the newspaper or what? I mean you don't look like a small town kid – unless small town kids are doing their shopping in Paris nowadays."

"You'd be surprised what kind of stuff comes into towns like this," she said, with a little smile breaking through the tension in her face. "And I'm not a kid..."

"OK, you're not a kid," he agreed. "Now maybe you can answer my question."

She wrinkled up her nose in a look of annoyance and glanced away, breaking eye contact with him. "I came here from Chicago," she said. "I'd done some graduate work in journalism and had come across a magazine article about the Mannings – Felix and Elizabeth..." Her voice started to break.

"Go on," he said, brusquely. "Finish what you have to say and save your tears for the end."

This time he saw a spark of fire in her eyes. But her voice was restrained. "I was really fascinated by the article because I was so fed up with what the media had become and here were two people going back to the basics ..." She fingered her tiny cigar and stared past him.

"Back to their roots, huh?" he said, with ill-disguised sarcasm.

"Something like that..."

"Felix came from Boston and was an art historian. He wrote about museums. Elizabeth grew up in Berkeley near – San Francisco – and went to a posh girl's school in Oakland. She was an illustrator – a graphics designer. Did you know that?"

She shook her head.

"You call starting a newspaper in a backwoods farming town going back to their roots?"

"Metaphorically speaking..."

"I hope you don't use words like that on the street here,"

he said. "People are liable to wash your mouth out with moonshine..."

"People here are smarter than you might think," she said.

"So you read about them in a magazine article," he continued, ignoring her last remark, "and decided that the idea of two high flyers from the city cranking out a little newspaper in the woods appealed to you..."

"What appealed to me, Mr. Radkin, was the idea of people bringing journalism back into the communities, revitalising the traditions which once made American newspapers great, not that that seems to matter much to you. Anyway, I wrote them and said I admired what they were trying to do and wondered if I could work with them for a while, as an intern ..."

"And they wrote back?"

She nodded and took another puff at her cheroot. "They were delighted. They said they could use the help but they couldn't offer me a salary – just a place to stay."

"Where was that?"

"Here in the newspaper office," she said. "There's a room off the back of the print shop. It's not fancy, but it's better than the dorms in Chicago."

"No salary, huh?" He glanced at her skinny frame. "How do you get by?"

"I've got some money of my own," she said, somewhat defensively.

"A real community press," he muttered, pouring himself another drink, "run by three outsiders with money to burn."

"Look here, Radkin!" she said, standing up and putting her hands on her wasplike waist. "I've had about as much as I can take! I said I had money of my own. I meant I had some savings. Money hard earned, I might add. And anyway, what's it to you? What makes you so fucking selfrighteous?"

"Go ahead, sit down," he said, grinning at her wide enough to show his nicotine-stained teeth. "I'm just shooting off my mouth, that's all." He pointed to the bottle. "It's the whisky."

She folded her arms and stood her ground. "You're a

schmuck, you know that?"

"Of course, I'm a schmuck. Everyone's a schmuck in this racket. You'll be a schmuck, too, if you stay at it long enough. Go ahead, sit down," he said, motioning to her chair. "We got work to do that is, if you still want to help."

Hesitating a moment, she finally sat back down. "What do you want to know?" she grumbled.

"Whatever you got to tell me about the murder case they were working on."

"It was Elizabeth's story more than Felix's," she said. "She was the one who kept pressing for it to go ahead..."

He rubbed the side of his face, feeling the length of his bristles. "That's strange," he replied. "She seemed to indicate that he was the one getting all the flak."

"People saw him as the publisher. He was the man, after all."

"But she said he was getting very secretive." He gave her a questioning look. "Did you notice any change in him over the last few days?"

"Like I said, I was only here a month," she replied. "He always seemed busy and in a rush. But he was kind – he usually had time to say a few words to me, even if it was only to ask if I was doing OK. I really didn't see him much over the last week. So I couldn't say whether there was any change in him since he wasn't around..."

"How about Elizabeth? Did she take you into her confidence? I mean, did she talk to you about him?"

She shook her head. "Not much. I was just settling in. She often seemed preoccupied, though..."

"What was your job around here?" he asked.

"Mostly office stuff. Answering the phone, filing. Elizabeth was training me to set type..."

"So you were sort of a girl Friday?

She crossed her legs and put her chin in her hand, taking on the pose she had when he saw her on the rock. "I guess you could say that."

"Any strange phone calls?"

"Yeah, there were some strange phone calls. But nothing particularly threatening..."

He lit another cigarette and smoked about half of it, silently trying to size her up. Then he said, "What do you think?"

She looked at him with surprise. "You're asking me?"

"That's right, I'm asking you. I figure maybe you have an opinion."

"I do," she said, looking at him seriously. "I think they were murdered..."

"What makes you say that?" he asked.

She shrugged. "Lots of weird people here..."

"Lots of weird people everywhere," he replied.

"This isn't your ordinary small town, Radkin. Half the people seem to be from another planet..."

He wondered what planet she was from, herself, as he leaned down and shoved the magazines off the table. "Bring over some paper, will you?" he asked, lighting up another cigarette while she went to oblige.

She came back with some yellow ruled pads which she had pulled from the front desk and a box of newly sharpened pencils. He took a pencil from the box, held it up and inspected the point.

"Very nice," he said. "Is that what they taught you in newspaper school?"

"Yeah," she replied. "They taught us to make them good and pointy so it's easier to stick up someone's butt."

"I hope your eyes are as good as your mouth," he said. "Let's start making a list of names, events and places. I want to know about everything that went through this office in the last month."

"Everything?"

"Everything! People, dogs, sneezes. If a worm crawled through the door, I want to know about it."

"A worm?"

"Yes. Especially if it was packing a flamethrower..."

31

Chapter 5

HE HAD GONE through all the back issues of the Gazette published since the Mannings had taken over without coming up with anything he could sink his teeth into. Sure there were bits and pieces of information, but nothing that could give him that spark of intuition he felt he needed.

In his way of thinking, facts were far less important than ideas. Facts were excess commodities; they existed in vast, uncountable units like grains of sand. And, like grains of sand, you could sift through them for eternity without accomplishing much more than the act of sifting.

Ideas were something else. They provided the skeleton which gave facts a substance – someplace to stick themselves onto. Without ideas, facts were just bits of matter which had no inherent meaning. Yet the development of ideas depended on sorting through facts. How this circular process worked was something of a mystery. But if a story really mattered, it soon became much more than a story. It became a quest for that unifying notion which put it all together for him.

If that happened, if everything fell into place, if he felt that special buzz which electrified his body, then he knew he was on to something. And he felt alive again. He hadn't felt that way for a long time. And he wasn't sure he felt that way now.

He thought about this as he paged through the Manning's files late that night wondering why he stayed and why he didn't just hop in his car and go back home. He didn't owe anything to anyone except his wife and kids. And he had messed that up. But he certainly didn't owe anything to Elizabeth and Felix. Sure, he wanted to know what happened to them – to her. But he didn't owe her anything.

On the other hand, he thought, she did ask him to help.

And he said he would, even though he regretted saying it. But he hadn't been able to do anything for her. She died a horrible death and she was someone he cared about, even if he had a hard time admitting it. He didn't think he owed her anything. But maybe he did.

And maybe that's why he had stayed around. But what about Gabriella? She had only known them for a month. He had known them for years.

Watching her come in, carrying a hot cup of coffee, he wondered about that.

"Where's the current files? The stuff they were working on..." he asked as she set the coffee down before him.

"They had an office at home," she said. "Most of the current files were kept there. I guess they're all destroyed..."

He thought it strange that there wasn't anything related to the murder case Elizabeth was so concerned about. Nothing at all. Maybe Gabriella was right and everything was destroyed in the fire. But why was there nothing in the back issues of the newspaper? Unless they were saving it up for a major scoop. Maybe they didn't know how to handle it. Or maybe they were dissuaded. Wasn't that the implication when Gabriella said it was a source of friction between them?

"You want any sugar in your coffee?" she asked.

He took a sip and shook his head. "Who owned the Gazette before the Mannings took it over?"

"It was started around the turn of the century by a man named Henry Vickers. Ecstasy, I understand, was a farming village and market town for the mining and lumber people. There were only two newspapers in the county – here and Capital City. Capital City's focus was statewide politics. The Gazette was always local, directed to farmers. It was part of the Grange movement, Elizabeth told me. A pretty radical paper for its day."

"How long did it last?" He took another sip of coffee and looked up.

"Till the mid-50's, I think. After that it had pretty much

33

lost its base. The reason all the equipment remained is that somebody back then had the bright idea it might make an interesting museum. So they kept it in moth balls for thirty years till one of the great-grandchildren decided to sell it off. By that time all the original family had either died or moved away."

"Who's Silas Adler?" he asked.

She looked at him strangely. "Why did you ask me that?"

"There was a reference to him in that magazine article you gave me about the Mannings. It said Adler was the one who told Felix the Gazette was up for sale."

"He and Felix were old friends," she said.

"Adler lives around here?"

"He had a vacation home by the Trinity River. Quite a nice estate..."

"You know him?" asked Joseph.

"Not personally," she replied, avoiding his questioning gaze.

He scribbled down a note and then said, "There's also some references to a commune around here – the New World Church. Can you give me some dope on them?"

"It's run by a guy named Jeremiah Cross. They seem to be fairly self-contained. They have their own food supplies – their own cattle and farms. So you rarely see them in town. And the commune itself is fenced off ..."

"Why's that?"

"To keep people out, I guess."

After making another notation, he looked at her again and said, "Tell me more about the town."

"What do you want to know?" she asked.

"Who lives here, who runs – it things like that..."

"I've only been here a month," she reminded him. "I don't know much."

"I'll take what you got," he told her.

"There's really two groups here, as far as I can tell. The old-timers, the ones whose families go back a couple generations, and the newcomers. The old-timers are farmers or woodsmen or relatives of miners who came here about a century ago. If the town depended on them, it would be dead by now. The newcomers are either part-time residents who come for the fishing and clean air or people like Carl Mundt and Harold Grimes who came up for reasons I don't know. Maybe they just don't like city life."

"Mundt and Grimes? Who are they?" he asked.

"Mundt owns the only industry in town – a sausage company. He also runs the Alfhem cafe. Grimes has a curio shop."

"What kind of curio shop?"

"It's down by the river. Strange place. Mainly Indian relics. I've never seen anyone go in there. Frankly, I don't know how he makes a living."

"Maybe it's seasonal," Joseph suggested. "Maybe he has a mail order trade."

"Or maybe he deals in other things," she said.

"What other things did you have in mind?" he asked. He didn't like the idea of talking in riddles.

"I only said that because I'm tired." She seemed flustered as she stretched her arms and yawned. "It's getting late. I'm going to bed."

Chapter 6

THE FIRST THING he saw when he opened his eyes was a face leering at him with a horrifying grin. The teeth were encrusted with jewels and two fangs protruded, menacingly, from the corners of the mouth.

Sitting up on the couch, he felt the dryness in his throat. He looked over at the empty bottle of whisky and the ashtray full of smokes. That only accounted for some of the pain in his head. The deathly face which had entered his consciousness with such diabolical force seemed more to the point.

35

Curious he hadn't seen that ghastly thing before, he thought, as he walked over to where it was hanging. Underneath was a little plaque which read, "Replica of Mayan Funeral Mask, Classic Period, Guatemala."

He rubbed his aching head and wondered why anyone would want a funeral mask hanging on their wall. Life was hard enough without having bleak subliminal messages oozing through the atmosphere while you were trying to concentrate on work. You might as well set up office in a graveyard. The idea crossed his mind as he walked over to the business side of the room.

Still blearyeyed from lack of sleep and too much drink, he began searching through the file cabinets. Coffee would have been nice. A bathroom would have been nicer. But since neither seemed to be in the cards at the moment, he settled for a can of fizzy cola he found in one of the drawers.

Having lubricated the parchness in his throat, he made his way to the upright telephone sitting prim and proper on the desk, like a starched secretary with wire-rimmed spectacles and hair done up in a tight, little bun. It was the kind antique freaks like rebuilding with modern electronics while maintaining the aura of a time when you tried cranking up Mabel-the-operator only to find someone else from your four-party line had gotten there first. Nostalgia, he used to tell Polly, was just another drug – a way of taking refuge in the illusion of a past. But then, sometimes, he felt that life, itself, was an illusion of the present.

The idea meandered through his brain as he awkwardly tried to dial his number on the rotary device which sat at the bottom of the statuesque pole, realizing that in the twenties when the damn thing was built, people must have had thinner fingers.

Then it occurred to him as he heard the ringing on the other end of the line, that in order to punch in the code for his answering machine to regurgitate its messages, he needed a phone with push buttons on it. Grimacing, he put the receiver back in its cradle and spat out a curse which related to all electronic barriers the new world order presented.

Fumbling through his rumpled jacket, which he had slept in for warmth, he found his little black address book and opened it up. He licked his index finger, more out of habit than necessity, and rifled through the pages till he found what he wanted. Then, lifting the receiver again, he dialed the number with his pinkie.

"Enterprise News Service. Can I help you?" The voice was sugar sweet, charged with the kind of plastic aural-eroticism that desperate men sometimes pay good money for.

"Only God can help me, Harriet," he said, "and I understand she's on extended sick leave."

"Oh, it must be Radkin. You don't sound too good..."

"Let me speak to the boss."

"Tarzan said that if you called I should say he's not in."

"OK, you said it. Now connect me."

"I better not."

"Don't worry about it, Harriet. You can say it's his wife."

"He never lets his wife through either."

"How about his broker?"

"You can try."

"What's his name?"

"Sneed. Jim Sneed."

"Alright. Say it's Jim Sneed and I got a tip on the market."

He waited a minute and then a voice came on the line. "Hey, Jim, baby! What's happening?"

"Listen carefully and don't hang up," said Joseph.

"Say, who is this?"

"Felix and Elizabeth Manning died last night..."

"What?"

"In a fire."

"Shit!"

"It's possibly murder."

"Who is this?"

"Radkin."

37

"Radkin! Is this your idea of a joke?"

"I wouldn't joke about something like that. When was the last time you heard from them?"

"Not since the old days when we all worked on the daily. They just seemed to drop out of sight. What's this about murder?"

"Elizabeth came to see me a couple of days ago. She said they had moved up north and started a little newspaper. Said they were covering a story about a farm worker who might have been unjustly convicted of stabbing someone to death. Seems they had stepped on a few toes in the process. Threatening phone calls all that. She was scared she'd opened up a hornet's nest. Wanted me to come up. I arrived yesterday evening just after their house burnt down. Firemen found two remains. Probably theirs."

"Christ! What an awful way to go!"

"Fireman I talk to said it was the hottest blaze he'd ever seen. Sounded to me like it might have been arson."

"Where are you now?"

"In their office. It's in a town called Ecstasy. In Trinity County..."

"Yeah. I heard of it."

"You have?"

"McLean was doing a story about some fundamentalist sect that's been operating out of there."

"No shit!" Joseph's ears pricked up. "What's it about?"

"Can't recall the details. It was sometime back. But it had a Central American connection."

"McLean still around?"

"No. He left about six months ago. Don't know whether he ever finished the story. Nothing came through here, anyhow..."

"I'd like to stick with this see what comes up," said Joseph.

"You know I can't give you an assignment. Anyway, it doesn't sound like wire service stuff..." "

Might be. The Mannings had a following. Seems some

38

national mags picked up on their small town newspaper gig..."

"Jesus, I liked her! Can't believe she died like that!"

"So what do you say?"

"Can't send it under you byline."

"I'll do it as 'Charles Chance'."

"What does your bank think about getting checks like that?"

"They don't mind as long as it clears. Just figure I'm another dope dealer."

"Yeah. Well give me a call later in the week. And Radkin..."

"What?"

"Try getting your act together. You're too good of a journalist to let everything fall apart..."

"Maybe you should tell that to the rest of the world," was his response.

Chapter 7

HE WAS JUST hanging up the phone as Gabriella walked in, barefoot, yawning, wearing a long black T-shirt that went down to her knees. She was carrying a cup of steaming coffee which she handed him.

"Sleep alright?" she asked.

"Like a baby in a barnyard," he said, taking a grateful sip. "Where's the john?"

She pointed back, in the direction of the door she had entered. "Into the print shop and to your left," she told him.

He followed her instructions, did his business, and then came back, marvelling, as he passed, at the antique press set in the center of the workroom like a monument to a different age when words had meaning beyond the trite and trivial. Back then, he suspected, when type was set manually with a limited number of handcast fonts, you had to tell your story in the most straightforward and simple way. It was like making an aboriginal fire – you put in just as much wood as you were going to use up. And that was that.

Gabriella was leafing through the notes they had complied in the wee hours of the morning. "It's a lot of garbage, you know," she said as he came back into the room. "What does it mean, anyway?"

"Nothing means anything unless you know what you're looking for. And you can't know what you're looking for until you know what you want," he replied, finishing his coffee and then lighting up a cigarette.

Looking up, he caught a glimpse of the demon with jewelled fangs hanging on the wall. "What the hell is that?" he asked.

She turned and glanced in the direction of his outstretched finger. "Oh, you mean the funerary mask? There's a fascinating story behind it. The original was from a looted Mayan burial site that made its way into the hands of a Mexican collector. But when the collector tried to have it authenticated, the expert he took it to said it was probably a fake. So the collector sold it off to an American dealer at a knockdown price. Then the dealer took it to a curator at the Museum of Natural History who inspected it and discovered some tiny holes at the base of the mask – like a beard had once been fixed to it. Since he had seen other masks of that type, with similar markings, he was convinced that it was genuine and, because of its uniqueness, probably worth a small fortune."

"You mean a worthless object suddenly became valuable all because of some tiny holes?" asked Joseph.

"That and the curator's experience with other works of that type. In archeometrics you often don't have much to go on..."

"How do you know all this?" he asked, staring at her and trying to decide how a kid from Chicago who took her degree in journalism could speak so authoritatively about an obscure mask.

"Oh ... Felix told me," she blushed.

He looked around for an ashtray. "You going back to Chicago?"

"I'd like to stay around for a while. Maybe I could do a final issue of the Gazette."

He found a small, earthen ashtray with an Indian motif and flicked the end of the cigarette into it. He didn't seem pleased. "Any place in town that rents out rooms?"

"I don't know," she said. "Frankly, I'm a little nervous staying here all alone. Maybe you could sleep here for a while."

She gazed at him like a lost puppy. The kind that wags its tail before it sinks its teeth into your leg, Joseph thought. He looked over at the couch he slept on the night before and made a face. "A little rough on the back," he said.

"There's a foldup cot someplace. Sorry I didn't think of it last night. And there's another room in the back. Felix used it for storage, but we could shove the boxes to one side."

"I have my own way of working," he said.

"I gathered," she replied. "Don't worry. I won't get in your way, if that's what you're worried about."

"Maybe I could use your help. But if things start happening I might just ask you to get lost. Or maybe I'll get lost myself. I want to get things clear from the start. That way there won't be any misunderstandings..."

"So what are you saying?" she asked him. "That you'll hang around as long as it's convenient?"

"Yes," he said.

"Just like a man!" she muttered underneath her breath.

"Yeah," he said, stubbing out his smoke in the Indian pot. "Just like a man. What's the name of Manning's lawyer?"

"J.P. Haggerty. He's got an office in Capital City. Elizabeth also convinced him to do Salvador Garcia's appeal," she said, writing down the phone number and handing it to him.

41

Chapter 8

HAGGERTY'S VOICE WAS strangely emotionless when Joseph got through to him on the phone. Maybe he had sounded different when someone was alive to pay the bill. "I heard about it this morning," said Haggerty. "The police rang me up to see if I knew their dentist."

"Their dentist?"

"They wanted a copy of the dental charts to use for identification. It seems there wasn't anything else for them to go on except jewellery. But that's not enough for a positive I.D."

"How did they come to contact you?" asked Joseph.

"Someone must have told them I was their lawyer."

"Did you know?"

"Know what?"

"The name of their dentist."

"Not a clue. I referred the police to their San Francisco attorney."

"I understand you're also handling the Salvador Garcia appeal."

"I was," he said.

"I'd like to speak with you about it. When's a good time?"

"What's your interest in all this?" asked Haggerty.

"I'm a friend of the Mannings. I'm also a journalist."

"I'm busy today," said Haggerty.

"There's just a couple of questions I'd like to clear up. It wouldn't take long. Then I wouldn't have to bother you again."

"Maybe I can squeeze you in before lunch. Can you be here at 11:45?"

"On the dot!"

Joseph scribbled the time in his appointment book as he hung up the phone. Then he turned to Gabriella and said,

"What's the name of that juror who contacted Elizabeth about the Salvador Garcia case?"

"Mildred Pike," she replied, still perched on the arm of the chair chair, watching him work like a medical student observing an operation.

Running his finger down the list of names on the contact sheet adhered to the desk, he looked up at her again. "There's no phone, just an address."

"I remember Elizabeth saying that she had the number changed or something. I think she was tired of being harassed.

Joseph tried directory enquiries and found nothing listed under last name Pike, first name Mildred. Putting down the phone, he jotted the address on an index card and held it up to her. "You know where this is?"

"There's a map of the area in the bottom drawer of the desk left hand side," she said.

He leaned over, opened the drawer and found it. Then, stuffing it into his jacket pocket, he walked quickly toward the door.

"Hey!" she called out.

He turned around and gave her a look.

"You forgot something."

"What?"

"Me," she said. "Give me a sec to get myself dressed."

Chapter 9

MILDRED PIKE LIVED not far from town in an isolated cottage looking out onto the Trinity River. It was one of those places scattered through the backlands of the county that had a timeless feel. Built of raw lumber in a clearing carved out from a grove of evergreens, they sat quietly puffing out billows of thin, white smoke from their chimney pipes.

They looked like old pioneers with a story to tell – how they crossed the wide frontier, dug for gold and wrestled grizzly bears before settling down to a sedentary existence.

It wasn't the same as finding an address in the city, he thought, driving slowly down the country road, trying to read the numbers off the bread-loaf mail boxes, each bearing a red flag, like a little semaphore pole, sending coded messages – depending on its position – mail arrived or mail to go. But numbers meant nothing out here. The mailmen probably knew which box got a particular Sears and Roebuck catalogue whether it had a number or not.

They found it by asking at a tiny fly and tackle shop that sold fresh bait to trout-hungry fishermen who drove up on the weekends to cast about in the last of the wild rivers. The man there was digging an oozing mass of larvae out of some reddish muck. He was a bony geezer with a stiff leg and rough hands that stank of organic slime.

"'bout a quarter mile down the way," he told them, with a suspicious look in his eye. "On the river side. She know you're comin'?"

Nobody living a quarter mile away in the city would ask a question like that, he mused, as he got back inside the car and started up. It wouldn't make sense. But, then again, in the city he would never stop to ask. People lived in readily definable units, organized in grids and quadrants. You found their place on the map and pushed a button. Information was systematized in the city so it was easier for journalists like him to do their job.

They drove another five minutes. Then Gabriella pointed out the drive. It was covered with pine needles and extended in a semicircle beyond the overgrown hedge up to the cottage and then back again about fifty feet down.

Parking the car by the front of the house, he looked out at the rushing waters of the Trinity river and beyond to the horizon of snowcapped mountains. "Nice view," he said. "People back in Frisco would pay a mint for a place like this."

"Everything looked great when I first got here," she replied. "Now I'm not so sure..."

He stared at her curiously, was going to say something, thought better of it and started to get out when the door to the cottage burst open. A stocky woman dressed in a robe and flappy slippers stomped onto the porch. He couldn't see her face. Probably because it was obscured from view by the massive shotgun she was aiming at them.

"Don't even think of gettin' out of that automobile," she shouted. "Just start 'er up and skiddadle!"

The top was down on the little MG so there was no sense in rolling up the window, Joseph thought. So he stood his ground and shouted. "Mrs. Pike? You are Mrs. Pike, aren't you?"

"Who said anything about Mrs?" she replied, her finger firmly planted round the trigger.

Great start, Joseph thought. He tried again. "We're from the Trinity County Gazette," he called out. He flashed his press card. "I think Elizabeth Manning talked with you before."

It seemed to be the magic words. She slowly lowered her weapon till the muzzle pointed toward the ground. "Well, don't just sit there! Come on inside!" she commanded.

Chapter 10

THE GARDEN WAS overgrown with blueberry bushes and thickets of vine. There was an old, weary-looking apple tree that provided shade and a wooden barrel next to it filled with rotting apples. The place was thick with the sweet smell of fermentation.

They were on the patio which overlooked the river, sitting on some old wicker chairs that were weather-worn from frozen winters and rainy summers.

She poured them each a glassful of cider from a two gallon jug. "Make my own," she said proudly. "This stuff ain't too strong yet, so y'all can drink up."

Joseph tried smiling, ingratiatingly, and took a tentative sip. He once had gotten stewed on cider and it wasn't a pleasant experience. In fact, it took a week before his plumbing was back in order.

"Wonderful aroma!" Gabriella was saying, glowingly. "And a lovely tartness. It's hard to find that blend of sweet and sour in commercial cider."

Not another foodie! Joseph thought. San Francisco was rotten with them. All they could talk about was where to get exotic five-bean pasta or extra virgin olive oil pressed by real virgins. If it wasn't that it was sex. And if it wasn't sex, it was property values. It was enough to make him want to eat canned beans and live a flatulent existence of celibacy.

But Mildred Pike wore a fat smile of satisfaction. Gabriella's gushing had reached a part of her that Joseph had completely missed.

"That's cause I blend the Gravensteins with Weinsaps," she grinned. "Proportion's three to one. But the other thing is ageing it in a barrel made of cherry wood..."

"Ms Pike..." Joseph broke in.

She turned to him. "Just call me Mildred."

He smiled, professionally. "Mildred, did you contact Elizabeth or did she contact you about the Salvador Garcia case, that is."

"I contacted her about two months back..." Her thick brows grew heavy on her face, as if she were considering other implications of that question. "Didn't she tell you?"

"There's been a tragedy," he said, trying to think how to phrase it.

"You mean the fire? I heard. And I know it weren't an accident."

"How come you're so sure?" asked Gabriella, putting her glass down on the cast iron table that sat between them.

46

"'Cause there's some people hereabouts that don't want none of their wormy cans pried open and they seem to be willin' to do 'bout anything to stop it."

"Why's that?" asked Joseph, taking out his pack of cigarettes and offering her one.

"Nah," she said, referring to the smoke. "Can't stand 'em." Then, answering his question, she replied, "Don't rightly know. Wish I did."

Joseph lit up and looked at the roughly hewn woman through a smoky veil. She was staring back at him; he felt the strength of her gaze.

"No idea, huh?"

"Nothin' I'd like to say. You really work for the newspaper?"

He liked her. He felt this dame was OK. "I'm a freelancer. I knew Elizabeth some years back when we both worked on the San Francisco daily. She came to see me a few days ago and asked me to help her out on the story..."

"Strange timing, if you asked me," said Mildred, still looking at him as if she were trying to make up her mind about something.

"Yeah," said Joseph. He rubbed the side of his nose trying to inhibit a sneeze. Wild plants and his sinuses rarely got along. "So maybe you could clue me in..."

"Clue you in on what?"

"On what you told her."

"Where do you want me to start?"

"Just tell me whatever you remember," he said, taking a pen and notebook from his jacket pocket.

She gazed out toward the rushing river. Her eyes grew misty. "The trial happened just about two years ago now, over at the county courthouse in Capital City. Sixty-five years old and I've never been on a jury before. Not complainin', mind you. Just seemed strange. Remember thinkin' it wasn't much of a trial. Two days, that's all. Prosecution called experts who claimed it was his knife that done it – Salvador's

47

knife, I mean. Found a farm worker who testified he heard him admit it. Hardly any defence. They never called him to the stand. Seemed like an open and shut case. Except..."

"Except what?" asked Gabriella.

"Except I never thought he were guilty. Not after watchin' him sit there those two days, so sweet faced and innocent..."

"Then how come you voted to convict him?" asked Joseph.

She turned around and gave him a pained look that seemed to linger with the apple and wicker musk even after she continued to speak. "Don't think I haven't asked myself that question every day for the last two years." She shrugged her large, ungainly shoulders and her chest heaved. "Can't rightly say I ever figured it out. I felt the kid was innocent but the evidence said he was guilty. First there were three of us, then two, then me. I just couldn't hold out..."

"It happens," said Joseph. "Even to the best of us."

"Yeah, but it happened to me," she said. "And it didn't really hit till I got home that night. I'd sent an innocent boy to jail."

She stopped. It was silent for a moment except for the sound of the rushing waters and the rustle of the leaves in the ancient apple tree.

But Joseph had heard it all before. Jurors were a notoriously guilty lot. There was always that element of doubt, even in the most tightly argued case. With most of them it ended there – just a kind of gnawing, like a minor toothache. But with some it grew, like cancer, spreading from a tiny cell to a malignancy – that seed of doubt growing into full-blown certainty.

"I stayed awake all night running it over in my mind like those video replays on TV. Time and time again. In the morning I thought I was going loony-tunes, so I called up one of the other jurors, Eunice, the woman who held out with me..."

"I thought you said there were three," Joseph cut in.

"The other was a man. Mr. Bodger. Anyway, I called Eunice and she said she felt the same as me. She had cried herself to sleep, she said. And then she told me. She'd found out that the poor boy never even understood what happened. He couldn't follow what was goin' on and he couldn't testify in his own defence because he didn't speak the language..."

"You mean they didn't have a court translator?" asked Joseph.

"They had a translator, alright. But he translated into Spanish. Salvador's language was some Indian tongue. In fact, it turned out he weren't even Mexican, like everyone thought. He came from the jungles of Guatemala..."

"But certainly he knew some Spanish," said Joseph. "After all, it's the official language there..."

"Market Spanish. He knew enough to ask for a tamale. Not to follow a complicated trial. Even at the end, when the judge pronounced him guilty, he just stayed in his seat like nothing had happened. The translator had to say it to him twice, in two different ways, till he understood. Then he broke down and cried. I cried too. So did Eunice.

"After I spoke to her that morning," she continued, "We decided that maybe we could fix what we'd done. So we phoned up Mr. Bodger, the other juror who also had some qualms, and then we phone up Mr. Mott, the public defender, and asked if we could meet with him. The three of us went to his office and told him we had second thoughts about the trial and asked if we could change our vote."

Joseph could just imagine the three jurors asking the public defender if they could change their vote. He could almost see the look of disbelief on the lawyer's face. "What did he say?" Joseph asked her, wondering if she had brought her shotgun.

"He said we couldn't – that's what he said." She made a face which gave Joseph the impression she probably would have shot him if she had the opportunity. "He said you can't change your vote even if you thought you voted wrong. He

49

said it's like chiselling it in marble. You can't erase it once you're done. Then we asked him what were the chances of getting a retrial. And he said not without some evidence that Salvador was innocent. I said that we couldn't prove the kid was innocent but we were sure there was reasonable doubt he wasn't guilty. And he said that didn't apply no more. Once we convicted him, there ain't no such thing as reasonable doubt. Now we had to prove him innocent."

"But you didn't have any evidence he was innocent, did you?" asked Joseph.

She shook her head. "Nope, we didn't. But we sure as hell weren't gonna let that boy rot in jail."

"So what did you do?" asked Gabriella, looking wide-eyed again, elbows on table, chin in hand.

"We formed the Salvador Garcia Defence Committee," she said. "Met every week for a while just the four of us..."

"Four?" Joseph's ears perked up. "There were the three of you the reluctant jurors. Who was the fourth?"

Biting her lip, she looked down at the ground. "Don't suppose it matters none now, seein' that he's gone." She looked up at Joseph again. "He met with us secret-like. He didn't want it known. Thought it might cause problems..."

"Who are you talking about?" asked Joseph.

"One of the court translators. Not the one who translated at the trial. But afterward, he was the one who told Eunice that Salvador didn't know Spanish. He was real upset. Thought the trial was a farce. But he couldn't be seen meeting with us.."

"Afraid he'd lose his job?" asked Gabriella.

"I guess," Mildred said. "But workin' for the courts weren't his only job. He was part of that institute..."

"What institute?" asked Joseph.

"You know..." She motioned vaguely across the river. "That language place over there – the Marsden Foundation. I think they translate bibles."

Joseph looked over at Gabriella, wondering if she was

picking up on this information. Then, turning back to the older woman, he said, "What did you mean when you said the translator had gone?"

She didn't answer at first. It was like something else was running through her head. "Maybe you should ask Father Kinsolving about that," she said. "He's sort of been our advisor..."

"Kinsolving, huh?" said Joseph writing down the name. "Could you get me his phone number and address?"

Chapter 11

HE DROPPED GABRIELLA off at the Gazette with instructions to dig into the disappearance of the translator and to find out what she could about the Marsden Foundation.

Meanwhile, Joseph contacted Father Kinsolving and made plans to meet him after his appointment with J.P. Haggerty, the Manning's lawyer.

Capital City was about forty miles east of Ecstasy through some rolling country side consisting mainly of grazing land and small truck farms. It took him a little less than an hour to get there.

Like most county seats, it seemed to have no other reason for its existence than to administer everything the state and federal governments didn't want. "Everything else" seemed to fit easily into four box-shaped buildings that gravitated from the central square, in the middle of which stood the ugly red-brick courthouse.

The place had a slow, lumbering, heavy feel about it, Joseph thought, as he drove into an off-street parking lot. It was a nothing town where nothing usually happened. And when it did, nobody probably cared much anyhow.

J. P. Haggerty's office was in the Farmer's Insurance and Trust Building. The elevator was one of those wire cage jobs that makes your stomach feel queasy even before you get in. Joseph decided to take the stairs.

Haggerty and Burns Associates, Law and Accounting, monopolized the third floor of the building. Joseph walked into the reception room, announced his presence and waited.

In about ten minutes a man wearing steel rimmed glasses came out from an adjoining office and walked up to him. He was about six foot tall and slouched in such a way that most people would have thought he was six inches shorter. He was wearing grey slacks which were held up by grey suspenders that fit over a white starched shirt. He might have been thirty or forty or fifty. He probably didn't know how old he was himself.

"Radkin?" he asked, pushing the steel glasses down the bridge of his nose and peering over them.

Joseph nodded and got out of his chair. He was about to extend a hand when Haggerty turned abruptly on his heels and shuffled off back to his office leaving Joseph standing there.

An instant later, Haggerty stuck his head out the open door. "I thought you wanted to speak to me," he said.

Joseph blinked his eyes and followed.

Haggerty's office was large and spacious, with shelves of expensive leather-bound books taking up an entire wall. It was what you'd expect to see in a corporate law firm on Madison Avenue or Montgomery Street, but not particularly in a sleazebag town.

"You wanted to talk to me about the Mannings," Haggerty said, getting into position behind his enormous oak desk. Probably a phallic substitute, Joseph thought, as there was hardly a bulge by Haggerty's crotch.

"Right," Joseph replied, finding a padded chair and sitting down. "How long had you represented them?"

"Just since they moved to Ecstasy," he said. "It wasn't all

that long ago..."

"Did you have anything to do with helping them buy the Gazette?"

"I looked over the contract and advised them."

"Then I guess you know Mr. Adler."

"Silas Adler and I go back quite some years."

"Did you represent them on any other matters?"

"Just matters pertaining to their work and their house. They have an attorney in San Francisco who'll be handling their will once the bodies have been identified, of course."

"What if the bodies can't be identified?"

"We'll have to wait for a ruling by the coroner."

"Did either Elizabeth or Felix contact you about threats made against them?"

"What kind of threats?" asked Haggerty.

"Any kind of threats."

Haggerty slowly shook his head. "Elizabeth asked me to help with the Salvador Garcia case. Some people around here might have taken offence at her interest in that."

"Why would they take offence?"

"Because some people around here don't like Mexicans."

"I thought he wasn't Mexican," said Joseph.

"Some people aren't as sophisticated as we are, Radkin. They consider anyone south of the border as 'Mexican'."

"Do you think any of those less sophisticated people might get angry enough to burn down the Mannings' house with the Mannings inside of it?"

"I wouldn't have thought so. But I wouldn't have thought a lot of things that people do these days. For instance, there's rumors going around that some carcasses have been found in the fields mutilated and drained of blood. Now who would get angry enough to do something like that?"

"If I had a buck for every time I heard those Vampire stories when I worked in the news room, I'd be rich enough to have my own hamburger empire," said Joseph.

"I said they were rumors," replied Haggerty. He made a

show of inspecting his watch. "Can I help you with anything else? I take it you're suspicious of the fire..."

"Aren't you?" asked Joseph.

"Wood burns," said Haggerty. "And shit happens."

Another philosopher. Just what the world needed, Joseph thought.

"Why do you think Elizabeth was so interested in the Salvador Garcia case?"

"I suspect she was a woman drawn to lost causes."

"Why'd you accept the case then?"

"I didn't say I couldn't help him."

"Listen," said Joseph, "I'd like to write something up about the kid. It could give a nudge to the appeal." Joseph tried to see if there was any sign of interest in his face. But there wasn't a flicker. "What do you think, Haggerty?"

"I'm no longer involved with the case," he said. "The Salvador Garcia Defence Committee and I had different ideas. My advice was to tread lightly."

"Why?"

"Because sometimes if you get people's dander up they might do the exact opposite of what you'd want."

"Are you saying if everyone had shut up you might have gotten him out?"

"I might."

"On what grounds?"

"Legal technicalities."

"Let me ask you a question," Joseph said. "Do you think the kid's innocent?"

"I don't know," Haggerty replied. "I'm not sure it makes much difference." He looked at his watch again. "Sorry to cut this short, Radkin, but I've got an appointment."

Joseph gave him a phoney grin. "That's OK. I was just on my way out."

Standing up, Haggerty said, "This case is really a minor affair, Radkin. I'm sure it's not worthy of your talents."

Joseph stood up too. "I disagree. Sounds to me like a

story that gets more promising by the second."

"Well," said Haggerty, "you probably know best."

"I might give you a call about the Mannings just to check on the I.D. You don't mind?"

"Not at all," said Haggerty, ushering him out. He said it straight, but Joseph knew his five minutes were up.

Chapter 12

OUTSIDE, THE MID-MORNING sun was the color of thin blood; lacy clouds floated across its path, filtering its rays. The temperature of the air was pleasant but the afternoon promised to be hot.

Joseph made his way across the street to the patch of lawn in front of the courthouse and sat down under a shade tree. He closed his spiral notebook, slipped it into his jacket and thought about his interview with Haggerty. What baffled him was why Elizabeth pressed Haggerty to take the Salvador Garcia case. He clearly wasn't interested. So why would he have accepted? He certainly didn't need the work. Besides, where did the money to handle it come from?

An old vagabond pushing a Safeway shopping cart had decided to set up camp under another tree on the lawn. Joseph watched as he carefully removed some plastic sheeting from the carrier and laid it on the grass.

Haggerty wasn't the type to do that kind of pro-bono work. Joseph would have staked his MG on that. And Elizabeth wouldn't have tried to convince him if she thought Haggerty would end up selling the kid out. So the only thing that made sense was that Haggerty pretended to be interested.

The tramp had emptied some of his stuff from the Safeway basket onto the plastic sheeting: a ragged piece of cloth, a piece of driftwood to hold it down, a battered replica of Buddha and a tin of something that looked like cat food.

But why would Haggerty do that, he wondered?

Opening the tin, the old man dipped his finger into the contents, drew out a chunk of what-ever-it-was and then offered some to the Buddha.

Joseph got up from the ground, brushed himself off and walked toward the tramp on his way to the parking lot. He reached into his pocket and took out a fiver. "Here," he said, handing it to the guy.

"Thanks, mister," said the tramp, grinning through his missing teeth. "I'll use it to buy a new Buddha."

"Screw the Buddha," said Joseph, walking on. "Spend it on something useful like booze or drugs."

Chapter 13

FATHER PATRICK KINSOLVING'S office was in the parish headquarters adjoining St. Mary's Church. It was a single storey wooden building with a sign in the window announcing a bingo game with the proceeds going to the earthquake victims of the latest shake in Peru.

Kinsolving was a youngish man with fair hair and an athletic figure who projected the kind of boisterous sincerity that usually made Joseph want to puke. In Kinsolving's case, however, Joseph sensed a modicum of self-doubt that made his exuberance tolerable.

"You're a friend of Mildred's? Wonderful!" he said, ushering Joseph into a kitchenette and sitting him down at a formica table. "What can I offer you? Beer? A cup of coffee?"

"Beer," said Joseph. "Thanks..."

"No problem," Kinsolving said, going over to the fridge and extracting two cans of generic brew. "I think I'll have one myself."

Joseph watched as he energetically popped one of the tops and passed it over.

"Mildred's quite a lady!" Kinsolving went on, opening one for himself. "They don't make her kind now – more's the pity..."

"Yeah," said Joseph, taking a thirsty drink. "She nearly shot my head off."

Kinsolving erupted into laughter. "She's got a reputation, old Mildred does. Once she found two punks stealing her firewood. She held them at gun point, made them strip naked, threw their dungarees into the Trinity River and forced them to crawl on their backside under a blueberry bush before marching them home!"

Joseph gave him a suspicious look. "You sure you're a priest?" he asked.

"You want to see my collar?" Kinsolving responded with amusement.

Since Kinsolving was wearing an opennecked sport shirt with a loud, Hawaiian design, Joseph would have liked to have taken him up on his offer. But, instead, he said, "Mildred told me I should speak to you about the Salvador Garcia case."

"That was kind of her," said Kinsolving. "You mentioned on the phone that you were a journalist. Why don't you tell me what your interest is. Not that it matters, mind you. It just might help me understand what aspect of the case I should focus on."

"Maybe I could just ask you some questions see where it goes," Joseph suggested, pulling out his cigarettes. "Mind if I smoke?"

"Not at all," said Kinsolving. "Actually I wouldn't mind a fag myself."

"How about starting with some background? Give me a rundown of the events that led up to the arrest," said Joseph, handing him a cigarette and then tossing over his lighter.

Kinsolving lit up and inhaled deeply. Then, letting the

smoke drift from his mouth, he said, "It happened two years ago on July 14 – that's when the body was discovered in a strawberry field at Priory Farm. One of the witnesses – a woman whose house looked onto the field – said she'd been awakened the night before by the noise of a car driving wildly down the dirt road behind her house. She said it slammed into her fence."

Taking another drag on his cigarette, he continued, "The police came about twenty minutes after the call – about 3AM. They found the remains of the car. It had been set ablaze. The tires were slashed and the windows shot out. They made their report and then left..."

"I thought there was only one cop in Ecstasy," said Joseph.

"Priory Farm is actually outside Ecstasy. The matter was handled by the State Police."

Joseph nodded. "Go on."

"They came back again at 6 AM after a camp worker had found the body of Jacinto Ramirez some 300 feet away from the burnt-out wreck. He was lying in a pool of blood. The next day, seven men from the farm labor camp were rounded up. Each of them were interviewed by Sheriff Larson..."

"Why Larson?" asked Joseph. "I thought you said it was being handled by the State Police."

"Larson was the only one who knew any Spanish. It seems his father was a missionary and spent some years in Latin America. Anyway, several hours later, Salvador Garcia was accused of the murder..."

"On what evidence?" asked Joseph, scribbling some notes onto his spiral pad.

"On the basis of Larson's interview. He said he was convinced Salvador was guilty because he paled and trembled under questioning. He was quoted as saying that 'an artery fluttered in his neck'..."

Joseph stopped writing and looked up. "He thought he was guilty because an artery fluttered in his neck? He actually said that?"

Kinsolving nodded.

"I thought Salvador didn't speak any Spanish."

"He had a very limited knowledge of the language. Salvador was actually a Mixtec refugeejust like thousands of others from Guatemala, El Salvador, Belize and the Yucatan. Like them, he was following the harvest up the coast from California to Washington."

Joseph jotted something else down on his pad.

"They're called the 'shadow people'," Kinsolving continued, "because of their slightness of stature and because they're poor as dust. They cross the border illegally to work in gruelling jobs that even the Mexicans refuse to take. They end up living in the most abysmal conditions. Most of them speak only their native Indian language rather than Spanish. They come here only because they're driven by desperation. Because of their size and their willingness to accept such dire conditions, they're despised by many of their Spanish-speaking co-workers who refuse to tolerate those circumstances any more."

"So what you're saying is that Salvador, being Mixtec, wouldn't have been supported by his Mexican colleagues. But certainly he wasn't brought to trial just on the basis of his nervousness!"

"They managed to dig up a little more than that. But not much. Anyway, the trial began about two months later and lasted two days..."

"What kind of motive did the prosecution offer?" asked Joseph.

"None. They just set out a vague notion of fighting between rival gangs of farm workers."

"Gangs? In Ecstasy?"

"As far as the prosecution was concerned, the motive really didn't matter. They just presented what they saw as a straightforward police report."

"Any witnesses?"

"Only one. He testified that he saw Salvador do the

stabbing. But when he first took the stand, speaking through an interpreter, he said he saw nothing. A recess was called and the witness was taken into the DA's office. When he came out and took the stand again, his testimony changed."

"Let me guess," Joseph said. "The witness was an illegal alien himself, right?"

"Sure," said Kinsolving. "Most of them are. In fact, during the cross examination, when the public defender asked the witness whether he was afraid what might happen to him if he didn't testify the way the DA wanted, he nodded 'yes'."

"And on that basis Salvador was convicted of murder?" Joseph shook his head. "It doesn't seem possible after having met Mildred Pike."

"That's the pressure of the jury room. It's strange how people react when they're placed in that situation. There are loads of theories, but in the end it still boils down to the tendency to follow the voice of authority even for the most obstinate of us. If the police say something happened, we suspect it probably did. Besides, the public defender wasn't the type to make a fuss. He didn't pursue any of the issues such as perjured witnesses – he didn't really bring it to he jury's attention."

"Why not?"

"I guess he preferred to use it as a basis for an appeal..."

"That sounds like a generous interpretation," said Joseph.

"Generous or not," Kinsolving went on, "the public defender wasn't a bad sort; like all of them he was overworked and nearly burnt out. He didn't really have the time or funds to research the case. Especially since the prosecution was pushing so hard for a speedy conviction."

"And why do you think that was?" asked Joseph, putting down his pen and looking at Kinsolving.

"That's a good question." Kinsolving stubbed his cigarette on his beer can, dropped it inside the keyhole opening and then stood up. "How about giving me a lift someplace?" he asked.

"Sure," said Joseph. "Where?"

"Someplace you'll find interesting," he said.

Chapter 14

THEY WERE DRIVING south on the highway, headed toward Redding, when Joseph asked, "What do you think of J.P. Haggerty, Salvador's lawyer?"

Kinsolving didn't reply at first, satisfied, it seemed, to sit quietly and let the wind rush through his thick blond hair. Finally he said, "Haggerty's got influence. He could have been a perfect choice ..."

He fell silent again.

"But?" Joseph prompted.

"But he has neither the time nor the inclination to do a proper job, it seems."

"That's what I thought," said Joseph, pulling close behind a twin-trailered juggernaut and then suddenly moving onto the other side of the road in order to pass it.

"We've found another lawyer to take over the case," said Kinsolving. "A fellow named Beekman. Sheldon Beekman. He seemed quite keen to take on the appeal..."

Kinsolving stared at the oncoming traffic with some apprehension. "Aren't you a bit close?"

"Plenty of room," said Joseph, swerving back into lane, as the juggernaut let out an angry blast from its airhorn. "Beekman – he's another local boy?"

"San Francisco lawyer. Now resides in Mendicino. Used to be involved in farm labor law. Now..."

"Let me guess," Joseph broke in. "Now plies the cannabis trade."

"It's the biggest industry there, you know. Two billion dollars worth or so they say..."

"Knew a man who flew it out," said Joseph. "They'd bind

it in bales, like hay. Drop it into farmyards down south for distribution. Pre-selected sites, you know. Someplace the dealers could get to unobserved. Sometimes the cows would get there first." He turned to Kinsolving. "You ever see a stoned cow?"

"Don't think I have ..."

"They sort of stumble around for a while and then fall asleep in the pasture, dreaming whatever stoned cows dream. But the milk they produce is pretty lively stuff for the next couple of weeks..." Joseph floored the accelerator peddle to pass a lazy tractor. The MG shot ahead and Joseph decided to try for a pickup about a hundred yards on.

"By the way, my faith doesn't extend to defying laws of natural dynamics," said Kinsolving, gasping the handle of the door for safety.

"This car manoeuvers like an angel," said Joseph, just avoiding an oncoming Greyhound bus by swerving in front of the pickup. "Don't worry about the sputtering, by the way. It always does that when I drive too fast."

"You might try keeping it under ninety. The next stretch of road is pretty heavily policed. Radar. Sate patrol. Motor-cycle cops..."

"Sure if it makes you feel better." Joseph dropped the speed until the indicator touched eighty-five. "So this Beek-man guy is taking over. What's his game?"

"He's made a bundle in the last few years. Guess he feels he can afford to do a little pro-bono work. It's Beekman you're driving me to meet, by the way."

"I'm not driving you all the way to Mendicino, am I? That's a hell of a distance and we're not even going the right way."

"No. We're only going another few miles to San Carlos prison. I'm meeting him there."

Chapter 15

SAN CARLOS PRISON stood as a blight on the landscape. A dark, sprawling, shadowy structure, it filled the area like a rhinoceros in a rose garden.

Coming at it frontally, all you saw was a vast, bleak wall with razor wire and guarded turrets with catwalks leading into the cavernous interior where the sun was banished along with celestial time.

Seeing it that way, you could almost forget that the prison was set in the middle of some magnificent countryside – green rolling hills dotted with colorful wildflowers and fragrant pine. It was as if someone had taken a painting of a sweet pastoral scene and covered it with excrement.

The town which had sprouted from this monstrosity sat in awe of the prison like a feudal village surrounding a Transylvanian castle. It was, thought Joseph, essentially a town in bondage – a company town. And like all towns of that sort, it was clear from the outset to whom and to what it owed its bread and its salt.

Kinsolving directed Joseph down an access road which led to a scattering of shops and fast food franchises. He had him pull into the parking lot of a bland-looking Italian sandwich joint, standing like a tattered waif among the plastic opulence of the infinite Hamburger Empires that spoke so eloquently of the culture.

"A little oasis in purgatory," Kinsolving explained as he led the way in, holding the greasy door open for Joseph. He motioned to a man with a balding top and a fringe of mousy brown hair cascading from the back of his head down to his shoulders. The man was concentrating on a newspaper while chewing into a monumental roll which oozed yellowish stuff from its sides. "Beekman," he said.

"What is that stuff he's eating?" asked Joseph. "It looks like a toxic wound filled with puss."

"I take it you've never tasted the delights of Philadelphia cheese steaks," Kinsolving replied, moving in Beekman's direction.

"I've never tasted gangrene, either. I don't suppose I'm missing out on anything."

Beekman turned to look as the two of them descended on his booth. His round face was clean shaven, but Joseph could picture it having a beard and shades in other days. Just as he could picture the pudgy body, now clothed in a rumpled green corduroy suit, wearing denim of institutional blue.

"Two priests today?" said Beekman, standing up and giving Joseph a suspicious look.

"I'm afraid Mr. Radkin isn't quite ready to take his vows," said Kinsolving, sliding into the booth. "He's a reporter from San Francisco."

"A journalist," Joseph corrected. "A reporter is someone who fills blank space with black lines from someone else's head."

"So what do you do?" asked Beekman.

"I fill blank space with black lines from my own head."

Beekman rolled his eyes. "You know what they say about editorial detergent?"

"What?" asked Joseph, as if giving the required response to the first part of a "knock-knock" joke.

"It makes everything white in the wash." Beekman folded his paper and put it aside. Then, looking at Kinsolving, he said, "I spoke with Dash, today. Great little investigator we got. Rounded up an expert who'll testify that Salvador's knife couldn't possibly have been the murder weapon..."

"Marvellous!" Kinsolving said, clasping his hands together in a victorious gesture.

"On what grounds?" asked Joseph.

"The knife in question was absolutely clean," Beekman explained. "Not a trace of blood could be found. The murder weapon punctured an artery. The blood would have shot out under enormous pressure, seeping into the workings of the knife. Even a thorough wiping wouldn't have been sufficient to have gotten everything out. The laboratory couldn't even find microscopic amounts."

"What about Hernandez?" asked Kinsolving. "Have you gotten him to sign a statement recanting his testimony?" Turning to Joseph, he added, "Hernandez was the sole witness who said Salvador did the stabbing."

"Not yet," said Beekman. "But we have an interview with him on video tape."

"Isn't that good enough?" asked Kinsolving.

"It's helpful but the courts don't accept taped testimony the same way they accept written documents. Besides, recanted testimony cuts both ways. Once you cast doubt on someone's veracity, you then have to determine when he was lying. In order to overturn a conviction, you almost have to show a smoking gun."

"Which means coming up with the guy who did it," said Joseph.

"Or at least presenting a believable alternative," Beekman went on. "Dash interviewed a number of people at the labor camp and got some leads."

"Like what?" asked Joseph.

"There's a man named Gonzales who disappeared right after the murder. Some of the people at the camp told Dash that he was acting very peculiarly. He hid out in the woods for a few days and then reappeared to borrow some money to go back to Mexico. Dash got hold of an address in Mexico city and is flying down there today..."

"You get money for things like that from the Church?" asked Joseph.

"You're kidding!" Kinsolving laughed. "Private donations – some large ones have come in lately."

"So what do you think the chances are of getting the kid off?" asked Joseph, glancing at Beekman's unfinished cheese steak and feeling nauseous.

"In the long run, very good. In the short run ..." He shrugged. "The course of justice runs like a giant turn in a toilet full of crap. Sometimes it takes a hell of a lot of Draino to get in unblocked." He gave Joseph a hard look. "What's your interest in all this, by the way? I'm a little surprised the San Francisco media machine bothered to send one of their honchos so far afield. I wouldn't think it's their kind of story..."

"I'm a freelancer," said Joseph. He never had liked lawyers much and if he needed a reason, he thought, Beekman was a good one.

Beekman gave him a blank look. "Then I hope you have your own printing press."

"Even the worst newspaper editor will look at something if it's good enough," said Joseph, finding himself once again in the position of defending something he only half believed because someone got his dander up. "And even if they don't want it the first time, they might take it the next." He met Beekman's eye with a combative look of his own. "Besides, there's nothing particularly seditious about this case, is there?"

"Sedition is in the nose of the smeller," said Beekman, whose own nose looked as if it had done a share of sniffing in its day. "But you didn't answer my question. What's all this to you?"

"Radkin was a friend of the Mannings," Kinsolving explained.

"Elizabeth Manning," Joseph clarified. "Their house was burned down just the other day. Arson, I suspect..."

"That's the fire you were telling me about?" said Beekman to Kinsolving who nodded his head. "So you're looking for a connection?" Beekman glanced at Radkin again.

"It's a possibility."

Beekman looked down at his watch. "I need to call Dash before takeoff. Is there a phone in here?"

"There's a booth right outside," said Kinsolving.

Joseph watched as the rumpled ex-hippy drug lawyer made his way out and decided it was probably true that a leopard couldn't change its spots even if it tried. Then, looking at Kinsolving, he asked, "What do you know about the New World Church?"

Kinsolving's face turned grim. "Bad news," he said. "Bad people."

"I know succinctness is a virtue, but I hope that's not all you can say about them," Joseph replied.

"The New World Church is a creature of Jeremiah Cross. Cross was a real estate broker and former alcoholic. In the early '70's he started up a commune for young people who were detoxing from drugs just outside of Ecstasy..."

"That doesn't sound like a total waste of time," said Joseph.

Kinsolving shook his head. "You don't understand. The commune, in fact, was a survivalist program based around an Apocalyptic theology which could be summed up in four words: 'The word is doomed'."

"How do you save people with that motto?" Joseph asked, while at the same time wondering whether most priests would find that notion objectionable.

"It's not people Cross was saving, but their souls or so he would tell you. Cross actually glories in this notion of world conflagration. He and his followers await the Armageddon with eager anticipation. In their way of thinking it heralds the Last Judgement when the terrible wrath of God is delivered out to all sinners, followed by the glorious advent of the new millennium, a new heaven and a new earth for those who have been saved, that is. However, the real issue isn't so much Cross's theology, but its application."

"What do you mean?" asked Joseph.

"Cross believes that the New World will be the Noah's Ark of the great disaster to come. Europe, of course, is lost. Has been for some time, according to him. His reading of the biblical scriptures led him to think that his mission was to convert the heathen races in America – those that remain – and bring God's word to them. He believes that the world is presently engaged in a great final conflict between God and the Devil. For him the struggle lies in Central and South America which can still be saved from the humanists and doubters. But his real enemy is liberation theology in Central America..."

"Or Capital City, I take it," said Joseph, giving Kinsolving a significant look.

"Or anywhere else. Cross has found supporters in high places. In Guatemala, particularly, he's had enormous successes. The New World Church has sent hundreds of its missionaries there."

"Unlike the Pope who sent the Inquisition," said Joseph, savoring the irony.

"We have a lot to answer for," Kinsolving replied, folding his hands together. "But this is five hundred years later. And the poor in Latin America are now being crushed by other forces in the name of another God..."

Joseph wondered whose God he was referring to, there certainly were enough of them about.

"I understand there's a linguistic institute that's based outside of Ecstasy. Something called the 'Marsden Foundation'. Mildred Pike said one of the court translators worked there."

"Yes," Kinsolving nodded. "Miles Tippett..."

"She implied that he's gone missing."

Kinsolving looked down at the table. "He seems to yes."

"What do you know about the Marsden Foundation?" Joseph asked.

"The Marsden Foundation is closely associated with the New World Church, though they try to argue that there's little connection. Its founder, William Marsden, began his career as a Bible salesman in Central America. His life work was bringing the word of God to all peoples, no matter what language they spoke. The institute has translated the Bible into hundreds of different esoteric tongues and sends scores of linguistic missionaries into the field..." Kinsolving stopped for a moment. He seemed to be trying to remember something.

"Anything else?" Joseph prompted.

"I was just recalling a bit of trivia Miles told me. He said the foundation believed that the exact date of the Second Coming was in their collective hands. They believe the blessed moment will arrive the very instant that the Bible has been translated into the last living language."

"How do they know when they've translated the last living language? Isn't it possible there's always another tribe out in the far reaches of the Amazon? Or a forgotten Cucamonga Indian living in a cave somewhere in the forest?"

"You might well ask," said Kinsolving with a little smile.

There was nothing priestly about this guy, Joseph thought. But he wasn't complaining. "Do you have any idea what happened to Tippett?" he asked.

Kinsolving shook his head. "He left rather suddenly sometime last week. No forwarding address. No phone."

"There's another name that keeps cropping up in my interviews," said Joseph. "Silas Adler. You know anything about him?"

"Adler?" It was Beekman's voice. Just returning, he had picked up on the tail end of the conversation. "He's dangerous. My advice is to stay away from him."

"You had dealings with him?" asked Joseph.

"Just peripherally. When I was doing labor law. He was a corporate attorney. One of the heavy guns International Fruit Company used when they tried to annihilate the Farm Workers Union ..."

"I thought all you attorneys save your antagonism for the courtroom. Don't tell me you don't chum around together at the club..." Joseph winked. He liked the look on Beekman's face when you gave his pudgy ear a tweak.

69

"Adler doesn't hobnob with the likes of me, Radkin. Or the likes of you. He's in with the big boys..."

"How big is big?" asked Joseph.

"How big do you want?" replied Beekman.

Kinsolving stepped in, the heavenly peacemaker. He looked at Radkin benignly. "You said his name came up in your interviews. In what context was he mentioned?"

"In context of the Mannings. It seems Adler was responsible for Felix coming to Ecstasy. I'm not sure of the connection."

"Felix Manning was a journalist, I take it," said Beekman.

"An art historian," Joseph corrected. "He worked the museum beat and wrote esoteric crap that no one could understand."

"Well that's your connection," said Beekman.

"What is?" Joseph found his smug look as easy to swallow as the image of slimy Philadelphia cheese on grisly steak.

"Adler has a reputation as an art collector. In fact there's a gallery in San Francisco that lists him as a major benefactor. The Cimi Gallery. It's right near the Federal Court House. Adler held a reception there the same time I was filing an action against International Fruit. I found out about it and passed the info on to the union. When the guests arrived, in order to get in they had to negotiate a mountain of rotten bananas." Beekman grinned at the recollection. Joseph waited for him to say something like, "Thems were the days!" But he didn't.

Kinsolving made a display of glancing at his watch. "Well, folks, it's showtime." He reached into a plastic bag he had brought with him into the cafe and took out his collar which he fixed around his neck.

"Super Priest!" said Beekman.

"All for the cause," Kinsolving replied. Then, looking at Joseph, he explained, "We're meeting with Salvador and then some of the prison staff. I'm trying to initiate a language program for the foreign speaking inmates. If you want, when

I see Salvador, I'll try to set up an interview for you. Would you be interested? It might help keep his spirits up. The poor boy has been under a great deal of stress. For two years people have been building up his hopes for an appeal only to dash them in the end. And then a few months ago word came that his father died. The news nearly broke his heart. But he snapped back. As they say the kid has guts. There's really something very, very special about him."

"I'm interested," Joseph replied, as he made his way outside with the other two. "But don't set a date. I'm not sure what I want to do yet."

"Well, let me know," said Kinsolving, stopping to shake hands. He gave him a look of concern. "And be careful. Those people who've taken over Ecstasy – they're a nasty bunch."

"I'll keep that in mind."

"By the way, there's something you should see before you go," Kinsolving said. "There's a grassy field opposite the main entrance to the jail. Drive by there on your way out..."

Chapter 16

HE STOPPED BY the grassy knoll, letting the engine of his car idle as he watched.

It was a curious scene. A camp had been erected, complete with tepees and tents. It didn't seem particularly organized, appearing, instead, to have sprung up out of nothing. There weren't any signs or any indication why they were there. Just one of those things best described as a "happening", he supposed.

But most curious of all were the people themselves. There was a stillness about them, a quietness. Their faces, those that he saw at least, were different yet very much the same. Dark skin, black hair – Indian in appearance.

They seemed to be patiently waiting for something to

happen.

For what? he wondered, as he threw the MG into gear and drove on toward the highway that would take him either to Ecstasy or back to the emptiness of his house in San Francisco.

Chapter 17

WILD IDEAS WERE swimming in his brain as he drove. None of them made sense, particularly. All he knew was that he smelled something rotten. And it wasn't his socks.

Just a day ago, he'd been taken by the primitive beauty here – the rushing streams, the snow-capped mountains. Now he was obsessed with the isolation.

In the city he had the instincts of a cat. He knew how to move through crowds and disappear into the anonymity of smoky cafes. He knew the jazz clubs and the North Beach dives. He knew the network of alleys that ran behind Yerba Buena. He knew the barrios in the Mission. He knew the powers that were and the powers that weren't. He knew all that like the back of his hand. There was danger in the city but he knew how to deal with it. He knew what to expect. And when the unexpected happened, he could deal with that.

But here it was like another universe. It had a fragrant green wrapping, but inside there was death. This wasn't his territory. He didn't know how to blend into the countryside. He was just a sitting duck or, even worse, a gooney bird. The kind that couldn't fly. The kind that was extinct because it couldn't survive in a hostile environment.

He was thinking of all this as he drove up to the brightly painted cottage that once housed the Trinity Gazette. He looked at the sunburst yellow paint that was so cheery yesterday and thought of the puss-filled sandwich on Beekman's plate.

Parking the car, he got out, went up to the porch and tried the door. It was unlocked. He pushed it open and went inside.

"Gabriella!" he shouted.

There was no reply.

For an instant he felt that strange sensation of pre-anxiety, just before the adrenaline starts leaking through your brain.

Then he heard her call back to him, "I'll be out in a minute. Wait there."

Wait where? he wondered. But a moment later she walked in, having come from the interior. She was dressed in slacks and a loose fitting top. Her feet were shoeless. Her hair was a mop.

"I'm going back to San Francisco," he said. "Why don't you get your stuff together and come with me?"

She shook her head.

"Why not?"

"I've got things to do," she said.

"I really think it's dangerous here."

"I know it's dangerous." She looked at him with disdain. "Anything that's worth doing is dangerous."

He screwed up one side of his face and rubbed the bristles of the other. There was an answer to that, but not one she would probably understand. "Maybe you're right," he said. "But if you want to write about lions you don't have to pry open their jaws and stick your head in."

"Well fuck you and fuck your lion!" she said, glaring at him. Her face was red.

It wasn't that he was shocked by her language, it's just that it was so unexpected. The only response he could make was to laugh. Which only made her angrier.

"Why don't you just go back to your lousy newsroom and stuck your smirking grin up the rear end of your computer!"

"I don't have a computer," he said. He didn't mention that he hadn't a lousy newsroom, either.

"Well stick it up your inkwell then!"

"Does that mean you're not coming with me?"

"What the hell do you think it means?" she shouted. Tears were flowing down her cheeks.

He felt like a rat. Sometimes that didn't feel bad. Sometimes it did.

"You got any whisky left?" he asked.

She shook her head, while she mopped up the tears with her sleeve. "You drank it up!"

He thought about asking if she had any denatured alcohol in the medicine cabinet but thought better of it.

"Then how about we go out for a drink and a bite to eat?" he suggested.

Chapter 18

THE ALFHEM CAFE was on the far side of Avenue B. It had a creaky sign swaying in the breeze that displayed a curious picture of a rusty cargo ship.

Joseph opened the wrought iron door for Gabriella and walked in after her. The place was dank and smoky and smelled of beer and sauerkraut. It reminded him of a haufbrau where he had taken refuge once near Munich when his car had broken down.

Even the female bartender looked the same. She had that grotesquely pneumatic appearance of an over-the-hill Brunhilde in a two-bit Wagnerian opera.

The cafe was filled with a boisterous mob. A long banner strung over the bar read, "Ecstasy Welcomes The Brisbane Fishing Club!"

Brunhilde seemed beside herself, sliding frothy mugs

across polished wood to a sad-eyed waitress caught between two fat-bellied men who, despite their state of inebriation, were still on the make.

"You ever been to Brisbane, sugarbuns?" one of them was saying. "Right as you come in, north on Highway 101, there's a sign that says, 'Charley's Used Cars – No Down Payment.' Now I bet you can't guess who Charley is..."

They found a table near the back that was as far from the fishermen as they could get. It wasn't far enough. The raucous laughter and unrestrained belches and blasts of wind knew no boundaries.

"You want to try someplace else?" asked Joseph.

"There isn't any other place unless you want to go out on the highway." She looked over at the fifty-year old men pretending they were boys and said, "I've seen worse, really. I once worked in a bar on the South Side of Chicago. These guys are pretty tame."

He'd been to the South Side and couldn't picture her working there. But he couldn't picture a lot of things.

"I'm sorry I blew up at you," she said, giving him a smile of apology. Her eyes lit up when she smiled, he thought. Too bad she didn't do it more often. She was capable of looking nice.

"Maybe I was being too rough on you," he said. "But I was serious about asking you to leave. This town gives me the creeps. You said so too."

"I said it was weird," she reminded him.

"So why are you staying? I don't get it."

"I've got my reasons," Gabriella said.

A few tables over, also set apart from the Brisbane crowd, three locals were drinking beer. One was dressed in uniform. He was the tall, lanky cop Joseph had seen the day before at the fire. The cop was most likely in his mid-thirties. The others looked to be about twenty years older.

Sitting across from the cop, and facing in Joseph's direction, was a corpulent man with a tiny mouth and fish-like eyes that swam around helplessly in his round, pinkish face. He looked extremely uncomfortable and kept dabbing the top of his bald head, nervously, with a paper napkin.

The third man, sitting between the other two and facing the bar, had the build of an ox – a thick, short neck and heavy muscular shoulders. His hair was slicked back abruptly from his forehead; the lower portion of his face was covered with several day's growth of bristles, giving him a dark, brooding expression. When he turned, momentarily glancing in Joseph's direction, there was something in his eyes – a hard calculating look. It reminded him of certain people he occasionally met in his line of work who would stop at absolutely nothing to get what they wanted.

"The bald man with the beady eyes is named Harold Grimes. He runs the curio shop down by the river. You know the Sheriff. The other guy is Carl Mundt. He owns this dump."

"Does that mean you wouldn't recommend the food?" asked Joseph.

"They pride themselves on their sausages. It seems to have made quite a reputation with a motley group of middle-aged men who wander up here from the southern part of the state."

"What do you know about those bozos?" Joseph asked, still looking over at the threesome at the far table. The conversation was serious, he thought. Not your ordinary mid-afternoon chitchat. The dominant force was clearly Mundt; that was obvious. Grimes was nervous and unsure. Larson, the cop, was wired up like a coiled snake in a tiny box. Joseph thought he wouldn't want to be around when someone let him out.

"I understand they came here around the same time," said Gabriella.

"When was that?"

"About six or seven years ago," she said. "At least that's what Elizabeth told me."

The session at the far table had broken up. At least one third of it, that is. The sheriff had gotten out of his chair and had put on his hat. He said a few words that Joseph couldn't hear and then he left.

The sad-eyed waitress came over to their table and Gabriella ordered the special – Mundt's Bavarian sausage with sauerkraut and boiled potatoes. Joseph ordered a ham sandwich and a beer.

"Poor kid," said Joseph, watching the waitress tread carefully across the beer-stained floor, her skinny legs showing through the pink rayon uniform. "Having to work in a place like this ..."

"She'll make good money tonight," Gabriella reminded him. "Anyway, she could have it worse."

"You mean she could be working in the sausage factory. At least sausages don't whisper lewd remarks in your ear." He stopped and looked into her eyes. "You weren't studying journalism, were you."

She looked down at the table, took the salt shaker, spilled some salt and made a design with her finger. "No, not journalism ..." she said.

"Archaeology?" he asked.

She nodded her head and looked up at him. "How did you know?"

"Your description of the mask. It was too precise, too knowledgeable. Even if Felix had told you the story, you wouldn't have remembered all the details without some sort of background in it. So what is it?" he asked. "Why are you here?"

The waitress was already bringing over the food. Quick service, Joseph thought. They must have had twenty platters ready in he kitchen. And pre-made sandwiches.

Gabriella brushed the salt drawing onto the floor. The waitress lowered her tray onto an adjoining table and then took one dish and then the other, placing them carefully in their proper positions. Then she smiled. "Bon Appetite!" she said.

Joseph watched her walk away. "Maybe I got her pegged all wrong," he said.

"Maybe you got me pegged wrong, too," said Gabriella.

He took a long swig of beer. "Why don't you correct me."

She took one of the potatoes and sliced it up. Dipping it in the sauerkraut, she brought it to her lips. She hesitated a moment and then put down her fork. "I'm working for an insurance company," she said. "It's strictly on the Q.T., you understand?"

"I'm good at protecting my sources," Joseph assured her.

"We had some information that led us to Ecstasy..."

"Information sent by Felix, I presume?"

She nodded. "Yes. With Felix's help, I was able to use the newspaper as my cover. At first we suspected it was a simple case of Grimes using his curio shop as an outlet for stolen artefacts. But it soon became clear that there was more going on ..." Her voice had taken on a hushed tone and she edged her chair closer to where Joseph was sitting. "It could be very important!"

"Maybe you could be a little more specific," said Joseph.

"I can't. Not yet, anyhow. But it's clear that there's some sort of a conspiracy between Grimes, Mundt and Sheriff Larson. They're up to something, I'm sure of it..."

"But you're not sure of what."

"No."

He shook his head. "Come on, Gabriella. What do you take me for?"

She opened her eyes wide, in surprise. "What do you mean? I'm being straight with you, Radkin!"

"Like you were from the very beginning..."

"No. Like I'm being now!" She reached down and opened her purse. Then she pulled out a folded sheet of paper and handed it to him. "This came to the office today. Maybe you should read it."

Joseph took the sheet and opened it. The message was

typed on the page with ragged lines. He noticed that all the 't's were slightly off-kilter, probably because the typewriter key was bent: "The 11Ahau Katun is when Ah mucen cab came forth to blindfold the eyes of Oxlahun ti Ku, Thirteen diety. With their countenances blindfolded dawn ended for them and they knew not what was to come."

He read it over and then, folding the paper, handed it back to her. "Does it mean anything to you?" he asked.

"No," she said, putting it back in her purse and then snapping it shut. "I recognized the word 'katun'. It's a Mayan designation of time. A katun is twenty years, I think. But I don't recognize anything else.

"You received this in the mail?"

She shook her head. "Someone slipped it through the mailslot in the door."

"Who was it addressed to?"

"Just the newspaper." She looked over at him as she tried cutting into her sausage. "What do you make of it?"

"It sounds like a warning," said Joseph, watching her struggle with he knife and fork. "Sausage a little tough?"

She was holding the sausage down with her fork, trying to slice it. "Seems to be a bone," she said.

Making a lengthwise incision with the tip of he knife, like a practiced surgeon, she slit the sausage open. She inspected her work and then looked back up, bemused. "Something's inside of it," she said.

"Maybe it's another message," Joseph suggested. "Should I call the waitress?"

"No. Let's see what it is first." She dug something out of the casing, still covered with bits of fat, and brushed it off with the blade of the knife. Then she held it out.

It was clear to him that she didn't recognize what it was.

"Put it down!" he said.

"What?" She still didn't understand. Somehow it hadn't penetrated her consciousness.

"Put it down!" he said again.

And then she saw. He could tell by the sudden expression of disbelief that came over her face. It was a human finger, perfectly formed, if slightly shrivelled, with a yellowish nail pointing from the tip.

She stared at it in horror and then closed her eyes. It dropped from her hand as she fainted and fell to the floor.

Chapter 19

THE WALLS OF Mundt's office were covered with panoramic photos of jungle terrain, ancient ruins and peasant villages. Most of the photos had European men in the foreground, dressed in tropical outfits white suits, Panama hats – looking hot, but still pleased with themselves. One photo showed Mundt standing by a flowering coffee tree, proudly displaying the ripened berries in his hand.

Mundt was by his desk, talking with Sheriff Larson when Joseph came in.

"Pull up a chair," said Mundt, as he, himself, took a seat behind his desk.

Joseph sat down and shot a glance in Larson's direction. Larson was standing by the window, trapping flies in his hand. He looked to Joseph like a cop he had once known down south who enjoyed squashing insects with his thumb while denying he ever used force to extract confessions from prisoners with faces that had somehow turned to pulp.

Mundt's tone was serious – concerned but not apologetic. "I've checked with the foreman at the sausage plant," he said. "No one's lost a finger. There's been no accidents reported in the last month. So the only thing I can imagine is that someone's playing a sick joke. Sheriff Larson will interview the employees. We'll get to the bottom of this. Of course, your dinner is on the house. So are the drinks."

"I'm afraid that's not good enough," said Joseph, switching his focus from the wiry sheriff to the bull-necked man and trying to figure out how to make this opportunity work for him. "Miss Luna ordered one of your sausages and in it she found, not prime pork and special seasonings, but a severed human finger. What would you have said if she had eaten it?"

"It wouldn't have hurt her," said Mundt.

"Maybe or maybe not," Joseph replied. "But think about it – you would have been responsible for an act of cannibalism."

Sheriff Larson opened the venetian blinds from the window that looked out onto the street. "That your car parked over by the newspaper office?" he asked.

"Yeah," said Joseph. "What about it?"

Turning back around, Larson had a mean little smile on his face. "You're parked in a restricted zone."

"Restricted to what?"

"Restricted to real cars with real tops. You got a driver's license?"

"Hey what are you trying to pull?" asked Joseph, looking from Larson to Mundt.

"I'm asking if you have a driver's license," Larson repeated.

"Of course I have a driver's license!" Joseph said. "Why wouldn't I have one?"

Larson held out his hand. "Let's see it."

"Come on," said Joseph. "You don't really want to play this game, do you? I'm a member of the press..."

"What paper do you work for?"

"Lot's of them. I freelance. You want to see my credentials?"

The Sheriff's hand was still extended. "I want to see your driver's license, mister."

Joseph looked back at Mundt who seemed to be watching the scene with amusement. "I thought you wanted to resolve

81

this amicably," he said.

"I do," Mundt replied. "But Sheriff Larson informed me that a car like yours was recently used in a hold up. He just needs to check it out. Give him your license and he'll be on his way."

Muttering under his breath, Joseph took out his wallet and extracted his driver's license with the picture Polly had referred to as "the shit-eating grin" and handed it to the sheriff.

"When you're finished doing your little check, could you wipe off the grease before you hand it back? You'll find there's a few outstanding parking tickets. You'll also be advised to remember that the Supreme Court has ruled liability for that particular offence is limited to civil action."

"Nice mug shot," said Larson, glancing at the photograph. Then, sticking the license into his shirt pocket, he left.

When Larson had gone, Mundt took a box from his desk, opened it and offered Joseph a cigar – a big, fat Havana. Joseph shook his head so Mundt lit one up for himself.

"Look, Radkin," he said, "I can see you're a man of the world. I'd like to settle this without any hard feelings. But we've got a reputation to uphold and we wouldn't want anything to get in the way of that..."

Joseph noticed that a big blue vein in Mundt's neck bulged out as he spoke so it wasn't clear how these words were meant. Whichever way they were meant, Mundt looked threatening when he said it.

"You staying around for a while?" Mundt asked, clearly preferring the answer to be in the negative.

"Maybe," Joseph replied.

"Why don't you let us pay for your expenses. There's a nice Holiday Inn just down the highway about ten miles. Swimming pool, sauna, all the modern conveniences..."

"Thanks," said Joseph. "I prefer to make my own arrangements."

"Suit yourself," said Mundt. "But while you're here, the

Alfhem is yours. Anything you want food, drink whatever you want it's on the house..."

"I'm more interested in having my license back. I don't like feeling under threat just because I'm asking questions..."

"I don't see any problem with that," said Mundt.

Implied consent, thought Joseph. It was a concept that cut both ways and usually got him into trouble.

"Ecstasy is a decent town, Radkin," Mundt continued. "Decent folk live here. They don't like disruptions. But they've got nothing to hide."

"Fine," said Joseph. "Then why try to roust me like that?"

Mundt put his hand on Joseph's shoulder and gave it a firm squeeze. "I spent a lot of years building up a reputation," he said. "I wouldn't want to think you'd ruin it just because someone played a crazy joke."

"I'm not about to write a story based on a crazy joke," said Joseph.

"Good," said Mundt. He let go of Joseph's arm. "We're in agreement then."

He accompanied Joseph from the office to the door of the cafe where Gabriella was waiting. "I'm glad we were able to sort this out," he said.

"Yeah," said Joseph. "Real chummy-like."

Mundt opened the door for them. Above their heads, the sign with the little ship was creaking in the breeze.

"I wanted to ask you about that," said Joseph, pointing to the sign. "'Alfhem' is that a German name?"

"No," said Mundt. "It's Swedish."

"You sailed in the Swedish navy?" asked Joseph.

"Not the Swedish navy, no. It's just a ship I happen to be interested in."

"Ships and sausages," said Joseph. "An intriguing combination."

Mundt looked anxious to get back inside. "Enjoy your stay," he said.

"As long as you keep your ape under restraint, I'm sure

I will," Joseph replied, taking Gabriella by the arm. As he did so, she suddenly gasped. "Oh, no!" Her face had turned absolutely white.

"What's wrong?" he asked.

"My purse! I've left it inside!"

"No need to panic," said Joseph, looking at her curiously.

As they turned to go back, the sad-eyed waitress appeared at the door. She held up Gabriella's black leather bag.

There was an expression of immense relief on Gabriella's face as she quickly took the bag from the waitress's outstretched hand. "Thanks very much!" she said.

"I'm really sorry," the waitress said. "I'm sorry for everything..."

Chapter 20

ON THE WAY back to the Gazette, Joseph suggested they stop at the market for a bottle of Wild Turkey. Gabriella seemed nervous. "I'll meet you back at the office," she said. Holding onto her arm, he insisted. "Come on. I'll buy you some chocolate."

"I don't like chocolate," she argued.

"Then I'll buy you something you do like," he replied, pulling her inside with him.

She didn't look pleased; she cast a dour shadow standing at the counter, next to him, as he paid for his whiskey.

"What's it to be?" he asked, looking back at her. "What strikes your fancy? Lemon tarts? Pecan pralines? Saltwater toffee? Bubble gum?"

"Nothing," she said. "Really. I just want to go back and go to bed."

The clerk, a matronly-looking woman, glanced at him

and then her and raised her eyebrows.

She was quiet as they walked the hundred yards to the yellow sunburst cottage. It was only after she had unlocked the door and entered the office that she said, "I'm going to sleep. I'll talk to you later."

He watched her move toward the print shop door. "Wait a second," he said.

She stopped and turned to him. Her face was blank, expressionless as the first time he had met her. "What do you want?" she asked.

Pointing to her purse, which she clutched tightly in her hand, he said, "I'd like to see that note again..."

"Now?" she asked, with annoyance. "Can't it wait?"

"No," said Joseph, moving toward her. "It can't wait. I'd like to see it again, if you don't mind."

"I do mind," she said. "I'm tired..." She turned around and opened the print shop door.

He came up behind her and grabbed her arm. "I'd like to see it now!"

Swivelling around, angrily, she spat. "Keep your grubby paws off, Radkin!" Then, making her right hand into a fist, she tried punching him in the stomach.

He caught her punch in mid-flight and, in the same motion, twisted her arm.

"Ow!" she shouted. "You're hurting me!" She tried pulling away, but, as she did, her bag dropped.

Quickly, he bent down and retrieved it.

"Give me that, Radkin! Goddamn it! Do you hear?"

He opened it up and emptied it out on the desk. She tried to stop him, but it was too late.

Picking out a plastic sandwich bag from the contents, he held it up. "Do you often carry sausages around with you?"

"So what?" she asked, looking at him defiantly.

"What's it doing in your purse?" he asked.

"None of your business!" she responded. "Why don't you just piss off! Isn't that what you want to do?"

"Yes. But not before I get some answers. Why'd you do it, Gabriella?"

"Do what?" There was fire in her eyes.

"Don't play me for a sucker!"

"I'm not playing!"

"You switched the sausages, didn't you. While I was reading the note. You had your bag right there. You held it in front of the plate. I know you did it. I just want to know why."

"I thought you know everything," she said, giving him a look of defiance.

"I want to know why, Gabriella. But, even more than that, I want to know where you got the finger. It's real, isn't it. I mean, it's not a plastic imitation."

"It did its job, didn't it?" she said, still seething with hostility. "It opened up the town to you!"

"Opened up the town?" he shouted back at her. "You little idiot! These men are dangerous! Don't you understand? People like that are used to protecting their interests! They're not dumb! They'll figure out what's going on!"

"What do you know?" she yelled. "What the hell do you know?"

"Maybe I don't know much!" he said, lowering his voice to a growl. "But I know enough not to be hanging around with the likes of you!"

And saying that he walked out.

Chapter 21

IT HAD STARTED to rain. It was that kind of slow, summer drizzle that falls in a mist instead of droplets. It wasn't even wet enough for him to put down the top. Or maybe he just liked the feel of the cool dampness on his head.

He was a few miles down the road when he saw a telephone box. Pulling over, onto a pebbled siding, he stopped the car, turned off the engine and got out. Then, walking over to the glass booth, he went inside, pulled some coins out of his pocket and placed a call to his home number. The phone rang and he punched in the code for his answering machine.

There were some messages, but none that he wanted. There were three or four hang-ups that could have been her, he thought. But probably not. If she had wanted to get in touch with him she would have left a message.

He went back to his car and opened the passenger door. Bending down, he retrieved a pack of Camels from the glove compartment.

The siding where he had parked looked out over the valley. The moon was bright enough to light up the mist, giving the air a sparkle. The houses in the valley seemed all aglow, like tiny Christmas parcels seen through a prism.

He lit up a cigarette and pondered the view. It really was beautiful, he thought. But why should that surprise him? Evil of the worst sort wasn't ugly at all. In fact, it could be lovely and seductive. Sensual, even.

He took out his wallet and pulled from it a picture of his kids. They were smiling like sugarplum demons. He stared at their images until it began to hurt. Then, putting the photo away, he went back to the car. This time he fetched the flask from his getaway bag. He unscrewed the top and drained the contents into his mouth. It wasn't much. Just enough to make him wish there was more.

He closed up the flask and tossed it back into the car. Then he lit another cigarette and looked out at the view. The longer he looked, the more the lights down below began to shift and redefine themselves till he no longer knew where he was.

Lost in time, he thought. And lost in space. And trying to make sense of the unknown. While everything you love or have loved disappears or goes up in flames.

The rain had picked up. No longer mist, it came down with darkening force as the clouds blocked out the moon and the silence gave way to rolling thunder.

He fixed the canvas top, got back in and started up. He let the engine idle and turned on the lights. In the distance, at the end of the bright path, was nothing but darkness. He put the car into gear and swerved the wheel.

Ten minutes later he was standing on the porch. He knocked at the door and waited. He knocked again, harder this time.

The door swung open. She stared at him. "You're soaking wet!" she said.

"I know!"

Her face was as wet as his. "Are you coming in?" she asked.

He shrugged his shoulders.

She reached for his hand. "Please stay," she whispered. "I'm frightened..."

There was an intoxicating fragrance as she fell into his arms. She looked up and he was startled by the beauty of her eyes.

"Will you stay?" she asked.

She drew him closer. As if drawn by magnet, he leaned forward and kissed her on the mouth.

Her lips were warm and eager and when he kissed her again he felt her hands reach under his shirt and press against his flesh. Her hair had changed color from black to fiery red.

"You will stay, won't you?" she whispered.

This time he answered, "Yes."

Chapter 22

HE WAS SITTING at the desk in the office when she brought in the morning coffee. She gave him a peck on the cheek as she set the cup in front of him.

Looking up, he saw her smile and felt worse than earlier when he had gotten out of bed. "Listen," he said, "about last night..."

She put a finger to his lips and shook her head. Then, going to the couch, she got up on it like a kitten, her legs tucked under her, and gazed over at him.

Cringing, he glanced down at all the doodles he had made in the last hour while trying to think out what the hell had happened to him.

"I wanted to tell you about the incident at the restaurant..." she began.

He looked up. Her face had a sincerity he hadn't seen in it before.

"While you were away, yesterday, an envelope came. Inside was the note I showed you and also something else..."

She hesitated, as if she found it difficult to say the words. "I opened it and something dropped out onto the floor. It was wrapped in plastic, just like the sausage you found in my purse. I bent over to pick it up and then I saw what it was..."

Her expression had changed. Her look was grim. She had that mixture of hardness and vulnerability that comes from being young and having seen too many things too soon, he thought.

"When I realized, I went to the toilet and puked. I was overwhelmed with disgust and also anger. I was angry at you for treating me like a child. And I was angry at myself for feeling so frightened..."

"Anyone would have been frightened," he said. "Most people would have run..."

"I was too angry to run. Instead, I went into my room and put the covers over my head. I lay there trembling. I don't know how long. Then, slowly, the anger took over from the fear. And I decided to do something. Someone had sent that horrible thing to frighten me. I decided to use it to my own advantage..."

He listened to her and thought he had misjudged her by a mile. She was tough. Probably tougher than him, though he'd never admit it.

"I went to the market and bought one of Mundt's sausages. I took it back and carefully undid the stitching. I emptied the meat and then I put in the thing that had been lying on the floor. It wasn't difficult once I set my mind to it..."

Once she set her mind to it, he thought, she was probably capable of anything.

"Then I waited for you to come back.."

"You knew what you were going to do?" he asked.

"Pretty much. Yes."

"It could have gone wrong," said Joseph. "Maybe it was Mundt or Larson who sent you the finger..."

"I thought it was worth the risk. Either way, it would stir things up. Once the pot is boiling, things start to happen. Don't they?"

"You should have told me," said Joseph.

"I was too angry at you," she said. "I wanted to show you that I was capable of making things happen..."

"I'm sure you are..."

"You weren't then. Maybe you feel that way now."

Maybe she was right, he thought. Maybe he was wrong about a lot of things.

"You said you were doing some insurance work," said Joseph. "What's it about?"

"I told you," she said, "we had information about stolen artefacts being handled by Grimes. The information came from Felix. I was sent to investigate..."

"What kind of artefacts are we talking about?"

"Pre-Columbian. Indian pottery and masks, mainly from Central America..."

"Had you done this sort of thing before?"

"No. This was my first case..."

"So you were just sent here cold?"

"I was sent here to interview Felix and to check our list

90

with the items he discovered."

"Couldn't that have been done over the telephone or by mail?"

"Not easily. Besides, Felix wasn't working for us. He was just an informant. I was sent to assess the information."

"And what was your assessment?"

"Certain items definitely come from suspect backgrounds. But probably any dealer in pre-Columbian art has some suspicious goods."

"So what did you report back to your company?"

"That I needed time to pursue the investigation. They told me to come back. I refused."

"Why did you do that?"

"Because I thought there was more going on here than I could report. The insurance companies are only interested in profit and loss. If a claim can be easily recovered, then it's all well and good. But if the cost of recovery outweighs the probable financial settlement, then it's not considered worth pursuing. Not to them, anyway."

"But why would it be to you?" He took a cigarette from a pack on the desk and lit up. He held the pack up. She shook her head. "Toss me my cheroots," she said, pointing to a packet lying next to the typewriter.

He tossed the packet of small cigars. It landed next to her on the couch. She picked it up, took one out, lit up and said, "Insurance companies sometimes hire young archaeologists like me to help them out. We have certain technical information at our disposal. When grants are hard to come by, working for them can help pay the rent..."

"Insurance investigation isn't your first love, I take it."

She shook her head. "Like most archaeologists, I'm very concerned about the problem of looting cultural treasures. So was Felix. He thought Ecstasy was the center of a major ring..."

"So why didn't he inform the authorities?"

"I'm sure he did," said Gabriella. "But the authorities

have been notoriously slow to get involved. It's the Bureau of Customs that usually prosecutes these cases and they need to be almost certain that a conviction will result before they'll step in. Often, they take their cue from the Department of State. If we're on the political outs with a certain country, then cases involving stolen property are delayed..."

Joseph inhaled the smoke from his cigarette and felt the sting in his lungs. The nicotine could kill him, eventually. He knew that. But he was pretty certain something else would kill him first. Something or someone.

"What you're saying, then, is that you're no longer working for the insurance company..." He let the smoke drift from his mouth. He wondered if she really ever was.

"I'm no longer on salary. I get a cut if any insured items are recovered."

So you do have some financial interest..."

She shrugged. "The chances of recovering a specific arte-fact that was insured by our company is pretty slim. I don't think we're talking about that kind of theft. In fact, that kind of theft doesn't interest me as much as the looting that goes on at grave sites and archaeological digs. The first kind of theft is simply items changing hands. The second kind is worse – much worse. It's stealing someone's heritage..."

She got up from the couch and came over to the desk where he was sitting. Running her hand through his tangled hair she whispered, "You understand why I couldn't tell you all this at first, don't you? I needed to feel I could trust you. You believe me, don't you, Joseph?"

He took another puff on his cigarette. He didn't reply.

"You do trust me?" she asked.

"Trust you?" An unhappy smile crossed over his face. "I don't even trust myself, Gabriella," he said, going over to the window and looking out.

The rain had stopped during the early hours of the morning. Now the sun was bright. The afternoon, he felt, would definitely be hot.

He motioned to Gabriella. "Come over here," he said.

She walked over to the window, where he was standing, and looked out.

Sheriff Larson was rummaging around by the side of the cottage. His figure was stooped. He seemed to be inspecting something.

"What do you think he wants?" she asked.

"Maybe we should find out," said Joseph.

Closing the window shade, he walked over to the front door. He pulled the door open. Larson was standing on the porch; his hand was formed into a fist.

"Howdy," he said. "I was just about to knock."

Joseph stared at him without saying a word.

"Mind if I come in?" Larson asked, pushing his way past Joseph.

"Seems to me you already are," Joseph replied, closing the door behind him.

Larson walked into the center of the office and made a quick inspection of the room, like a linoleum salesman trying to estimate the footage. Seeing Gabriella on the other side of the partition, he took off his hat and said, "Howdy, ma'am. Hope I'm not disturbing you."

"What do you want?" she asked, giving him a look that sent shivers down Joseph's spine but didn't seem to bother Larson at all.

"It's a friendly call," he assured her. Then, taking something from his pocket, he turned to Joseph. "I wanted to give you back your license," he said, handing it to him. "And to let you know we've solved that business about the sausage..."

Gabriella shot Joseph a quick glance and then, looking back at Sheriff Larson, she said, "What did you find out?"

"Indian guy, down at the factory. Had a grudge. Always drunk. Lot's of them people get drunk, but he was real trouble. Mundt finally got fed up and fired him last week. He was the one who done it..."

"How do you know?" asked Joseph.

"He said so. Was right proud of it. Thought it was a great, big joke." Larson had a smile on his face as if he thought it was a fine joke, too.

"Did you arrest him?" asked Gabriella.

"Sure did," said Larson. "Trouble is, he escaped. But he won't get far. I notified the State Police. I'm off right now to the migrant camp. We'll pick him up. Ain't no place he can hide."

"Why's that?" asked Joseph.

"'cause he stands out like a sore thumb. Big guy, tall, nearly seven feet. Humongous scar running from the top of his ear all the way down the left side of his face to his chin."

"Sounds like Frankenstein," Joseph said.

"Twice as ugly," said Larson, grinning once more in Gabriella's direction. "Just wanted you to know that we're lookin' out for you, Ma'am."

"Yeah," said Gabriella, "Thanks a lot."

Larson tipped his hat again. "Well, got to be off."

"Just one thing before you go," said Joseph. "Maybe you could explain something to me..."

"Maybe," said Larson, standing in the doorway. "Why don't we give it a try."

"This Indian guy you say messed with Mundt's sausages..."

"Yeah? What about him?"

"Where'd he get the finger?"

Larson narrowed his eyes. He looked at Joseph and then he turned to look at Gabriella. "Well, now, I guess I should have told you about that. You see there's a problem hereabouts that maybe you should know. There's some bad Indians on the loose. They've been doin' some pretty awful things..."

"Like cutting fingers off people's hands?" asked Joseph.

"We've been finding remains scattered over the fields outside of town. Mostly its animals. But we also found some human remains that looked like they'd been used in ritual sacrifices." He turned to Gabriella again. "Don't want to frighten

you none, ma'am, but maybe you shouldn't go out at night
– not by your lonesome..."

Chapter 23

"LISTEN," JOSEPH SAID, glancing down at his watch after
Larson had left. "I've got a few calls to make. Why don't you
go over to the Alfhem."

She looked at him in surprise. "Why should I do that?"

"See if you can make friends with the woman who works
there."

"You mean Big Blonde Bertha?"

Joseph shook his head. "No. The sad-eyed one."

"Plain Jane? I tried on several occasions. She kind of
backs off. But I know what you mean. She does stare at you
with those big, cow eyes always seeming like she wants to say
something but never able to bring herself to it..."

"Well, see if you can inspire her." He made a phoney
smile.

"What do you want me to inspire her to talk about?"

"Sausages," Joseph replied.

After she left, he settled down at the desk and placed a call
to the wire service. He asked to speak with Research.

"Research Department," said the sour voice when he connected. "All the news unfit to print and then some. Morgan
speaking. Remember the shorter the request, the better we
can serve you. Besides, it's almost time for lunch..."

"Do you always babble on like that or did I just happen to
catch you with your nose full of glue?" asked Joseph. "This is
Radkin. I need some info."

"Oh, Radkin. Are you still working for us?"

"Occasionally. Can I just give you a word and have you
plug it into the computer?"

"Depends on the word."

"'Alfhem'." He spelled it out.

"What is it?"

"Name of a boat."

"I can try tapping it in, but don't expect anything to come up unless it's a keyword to a story."

"I'll hold on," said Joseph. He made a few notes on a piece of paper while waiting for Morgan to respond. He only waited a minute or two.

"You're in luck," Morgan said. "Dateline, Washington DC, May 15, 1954. Headline reads, 'Swedish Ship, Alfhem, Unloads Arms at Puerto Barrios'. Story: 'Secretary of State, John Foster Dulles, announced at a press conference yesterday that a shipment of arms from behind the Iron Curtain had arrived in the Western Hemisphere in defiance of the Monroe Doctrine. A Swedish merchant ship, the Alfhem, which set sail at the beginning of the month from Stettin, East Germany, listed its cargo as optical glass and laboratory supplies bound for Dakar, East Africa. In fact, the freighter carried 2,000 tons of small arms and ammunition from the Skoda arms factory in Czechoslovakia. Its real destination turned out to be Puerto Barios, Guatemala. Mr. Dulles claimed that the arms were not intended for the Guatemalan military. Instead, president Jacob Arbenz Guzman, intends to distribute them to his supporters in order to create a 'people's militia' under control of the communists.'"

Morgan stopped reading.

"That's all?" asked Joseph.

"There's a ton of references cross-indexed under Arbenz, but nothing more under 'Alfhem'."

"Any of the old codgers upstairs likely to have been around in 1954?"

"There's Wilson. He's always talking about the great time he had in Mexico after the war. He's the Latin American editor now. You might try him."

Joseph got himself connected to the Latin American desk. It seemed to be a slow news day south of the border because

96

Wilson was only too delighted to talk:

"Not many people remember Arbenz anymore," he said. "He came in on the wave of populist movements that swept Central America in the wake of World War II. You heard of the term 'Banana Republic'? Well, that was Guatemala. Literally. United Fruit owned the place lock, stock and barrel. They owned the railroads and the telephone company. In fact, they controlled all Guatemala's transport and communication. Then, if that wasn't enough, in 1931 the law firm that represented United Fruit negotiated a 99 year contract with the government which exempted them from virtually all taxes and duties. So they weren't even taxed on the export of bananas, the country's major resource. That's like Saudi Arabia not being able to derive any revenue from its oil. And you know who the lawyer was who struck the deal? John Foster Dulles!"

"He was Secretary of State when Arbenz was overthrown in '54, wasn't he?"

"Right on the button, kiddo! Code name, Operation Success. One of the first postwar CIA coups. Of course, it was almost a fiasco. But they pulled it off. And the key to making it work was convincing the American public that Guatemala was a bridgehead for a commie invasion of the US."

"That must have been pretty hard to do with United Fruit running the show there," said Joseph.

"You bet your sweet bottom!" Wilson continued. "But Arbenz was into nasty things like taxing their bananas. So that's why they needed the Alfhem. Didn't matter that the rusty old freighter was carrying out-of-date rifles your average hunting club would reject. Or that it was a legitimate purchase by the elected government of the day. The fact is that the origin of the weapons was Czechoslovakia, loaded onto a ship that was docked in East Germany. And you gotta remember this was 1954, the height of Cold War paranoia. When news of commie arms landing on American soil was splashed over the front pages, it hit with as much power back then as the revelation that the Russians were bringing missiles into Cuba."

"And you're saying the whole thing was a setup?"

"I'm saying we knew about the Alfhem before it even left. We knew the weapons it was carrying wouldn't arm a division of toy soldiers. We also knew that Arbenz wasn't going to use them offensively. He wanted to protect against a military coup inspired by you-know-who. But we knew how to bait a hook. And the Alfhem was a nifty hunk of cheese manufactured in our dairy and graded CIA!"

He made a few more phone calls to contacts and was able to find out some other things. Like United Fruit may have owned Guatemala in the first half of the century, but it's heyday was over. Bananas were something of a monopoly back then, but now they were shipped and exported from scores of countries throughout the world. Like everywhere else, time had created its own changes.

The other "fruit" that Guatemala had produced for export was from the coffee tree. He found out that most of these plantations had been started by German planters, many of whom were deported to camps in the US during the war. That might explain the plantation pictures on the wall of the Alfhem Cafe, he thought. It could also possibly link Mundt with the CIA's adventures, since ex-planters often made the best informants.

But that was twenty-five years ago. Neither bananas or coffee was much of an issue anymore, he was told. The bottom had fallen out of both those markets. Every semi-tropical third-world country produced them. The problem was overproduction. Sure, the forest lands were still being cleared of trees and Indians. It was prime volcanic farming soil. Successive Central American governments had fallen over themselves, trying what the conquistadors had attempted five hundred years before – to force the Indians, at the point of a gun, into providing a stable work force. And, even now, after five hundred years of brute force, they still hadn't been very successful.

Drugs, of course, was the next logical explanation. But Guatemala wasn't the most important player. Cocaine was firmly in the hands of the Colombian connection. And the part of California he was in grew more cannabis on its own than all of Guatemala and El Salvador put together.

That left Gabriella's story of the stolen antiquities. And Joseph could hardly believe that a small farming town in Northern California could be the center of an international trade in hot pots.

He was mulling this scattering of information over in his head when the phone rang. He picked it up. "Gazette. Radkin here," he said.

"Joseph. This is Gabriella..."

"Where are you?" he asked.

"I'm at Jane's place. You know, the waitress. It seems she's quite happy to talk..."

Chapter 24

HE FOLLOWED HER directions, driving up the incline that was called Miller's Hill. It was the area he passed through when he had driven out to the Mannings the first time he came. He remembered being surprised at the collection of shabby houses with the little vegetable patches. "Tobacco Row" they would have called it down South. Here it was just called "Shanty Town."

There was the smell of fresh baked apple pie when he was met at the door by Gabriella. She ushered him into a box-like room filled with plants and cushions.

"How'd you get out here?" he asked her, looking around for the sad-eyed waitress. "And where's Jane?"

Gabriella smiled. Her face was flushed with success, Joseph thought. "It turns out we have something in common," she told him.

"She not another archaeologist pretending to be something else, is she? I mean one's enough..."

"It's mushrooms."

"Mushrooms?" Joseph looked at her strangely.

"Yes, she's an amateur mycologist just like I am. This is a great area for mushroom pickers, you know. The woods back here are full of them."

"I'm sure they are," said Joseph, glancing around and noticing a picture of a giant fungus hanging on the wall. Mushrooms were not his favorite subject. As a kid he thought they were something you nibbled on one side if you wanted to grow big and then the other to grow small. Even now he didn't trust them. He looked back at Gabriella. "How did you wind up here?"

"I did what you said. I went to the Alfhem. We got to chatting. One thing led to another and she invited me back to see her collection."

"She took off from work?"

"She had a break. She goes back for the evening shift."

At that moment Jane came in carrying what looked to be a diorama – a cardboard box in which had been constructed a miniature woodlands scene. It was hard to believe she was the same person, Joseph thought. Her eyes were glowing.

"I've collected seven different types of spores," she said, excitedly, looking at Gabriella. "And they've all taken root!" Then, turning to Joseph, she smiled. "Hello, Mr. Radkin," she said. "Are you interested in mushrooms too?"

"Only in not eating them," he replied.

"But they're so beautiful. Such an array of shapes and colors. I think of them as little magic elves, frozen in time..."

"Yes," said Joseph. "The only other shape that comes to mind is a nuclear cloud."

"Exactly!" she said, her eyes still glistening. Her hand moved across the diorama tenderly. "Within the tiny mushroom is the power of the universe. All the good and all the evil..."

He cleared his throat and shot a glance in Gabriella's direction. "I thought we were going to talk about sausages..."

Setting the diorama down on a planter table, her eyes once more looked sad and she seemed to become the waitress again. "Of course," she said. "Sausages..."

"How long have you worked at the Alfhem?" he asked.

She shrugged he shoulders. "Two, maybe three years. Time passes so slowly there..."

"Where were you before then?" asked Gabriella.

"I lived in the city. I came out there to be closer to the woods. But I needed a job. Work isn't that easy to come by out here."

"What do you know about the people there? Mundt, Grimes, Larson..."

"I pick up bits and pieces of information..." She looked at Gabriella. "They don't think I'm very bright. They treat me like I'm part of the furniture."

"So why do you stay on?" Gabriella asked, smiling back at her.

"Because there's no other jobs. And because I want to be near the woods."

"How long has the Alfhem been in business?" asked Joseph. "I don't suppose it's been a family operation handed down from father to son."

"Mundt started his business about ten years ago..."

"What was he doing before that?"

"He's always been circumspect about his background. I don't know where he comes from. But he and Grimes talk about Guatemala a lot."

"They were both there at the same time?" asked Joseph.

"I get that impression. Yes."

"But you don't know what they were doing there?"

She shook her head.

"Tell him what you told me," Gabriella prompted.

Her face had become more severe. He could see the

101

wrinkles on her brow. "After that incident yesterday, Mr. Grimes spent a lot of time with Mr. Mundt in his back office. I could hear them shouting. They were talking about having to move stuff..." She looked at Joseph as if to warn him. "They don't like having you around."

He felt a queasy sensation in his stomach but his face didn't show it. "I'm used to that," he said. "When they talked about moving stuff, did you have any idea what they meant?"

"I don't even know from where to where..."

"What do you know about the sausage factory?" he asked.

"It's a strange place. I get sent there sometimes to pick up sausages for the restaurant. But there's something peculiar about it. The place they make the sausages is real small. And they don't make many. But the plant itself is real big..."

"What's the rest of the space used for?" asked Joseph.

"Storage. But, like I said, they don't make many sausages..."

"And you don't know what they store there?"

"No I don't. But I've seen trucks come in the night..."

"To make pickups?"

"Mostly to deliver things..."

"What?"

"I don't know. They're all crated up."

"Do you know anyone who works there?"

"That's another strange thing about the place," she replied. "Nobody from town works there. Not that I know, anyhow."

"If nobody from the town works there, then who does?" asked Gabriella.

"Indians," said the waitress.

"Where do they live?"

"Out at the labor camp, I guess."

"You mean the migrant camp out on the highway?" asked Joseph.

"Can't think of where else," she replied. "There sure aren't any Indians who live around here."

Joseph made a sign to Gabriella, indicating that he was ready to go. "Thanks for agreeing to talk with us," he said.

There was a sudden look of concern in the waitress's face. "I wouldn't want them to know..."

"Nothing I write would be attributed to you," he said, cutting her off. "Anyway, there's nothing to write about yet."

"Thanks for agreeing to talk with us," said Gabriella, taking her hand and giving it a gentle squeeze. "Don't worry. No harm will come."

"I wanted to tell someone," she said. "I've had a bad feeling about that place ever since I started working there."

"We'll get together soon and talk more about mushrooms," Gabriella said. And then she followed Joseph out the door.

Chapter 25

THEY DROVE PAST the sausage factory on their way back to the Gazette. It was a large brick rectangular building set apart from a few deserted warehouses on a small access road which led to the highway. A big sign that ran across the top read, "Mundt's Famous Sausages."

Famous for what? Joseph mused to himself. Then, aloud, he said, "Not much indication of life. Not much indication of anything, in fact."

"Where do you think the trucks she talked about were coming from?" asked Gabriella, staring out at the loading bay, which was sealed shut. If there had been any activity earlier, there certainly wasn't now.

"You tell me," he said, putting the car into gear and driving on.

When they reached the Gazette, Joseph let her out. "I'll meet you here in a while," he said. "There's something I want to check out."

Chapter 26

THE MIGRANT CAMP was a few miles north of Ecstasy. Travelling up the highway, it was easy to miss. The meagre living quarters were conveniently set back from the road so as not to upset the tourists. Just a flapping clothes line full of threadbare clothes and a rubbish tip were the only landmarks Kinsolving said to look for.

Pulling off the highway, Joseph stopped the car and got out. The dust was still thick in the air from churning tires. Brushing the grit from his eyes, he glanced around and saw a small stucco hut set off to the side that had a sign on the door indicating it was the camp's administration office. He walked over, kicked the sand from his shoes and knocked.

Kinsolving had given him the name of Edward Saez as a contact. Saez, he said, was a social worker assigned to the camp who had been helpful in the Garcia appeal. It was Saez who answered the door.

"Lucky," said Joseph. "You're just the man I wanted to see."

"Not luck at all," Saez replied. "I'm the only one who works here anymore."

Saez was a roly-poly type with a friendly disposition who looked to Joseph something like a Mexican Teddy bear. He was boiling up some coffee when Joseph came in. Sitting him down at a table cluttered with a distressing array of official-looking forms, Saez poured him some of the scalding liquid into a metal cup.

"We don't have any permanent residents here like they do down south," Saez told him, indicating the meagre camp facilities behind him. "It's just a passing-through point on the way up north. Last month the place was overflowing because the strawberry crop was in. Now it's nearly empty. People have moved on, following the harvest..."

Joseph felt his fingers sizzle as he put his hand to the metal cup. He wisely decided to let it cool before lubricating his gullet. "You have any trouble up here lately?" he asked.

Saez's eyes were as brown as his skin. They lingered on Joseph's face a while. "There's always trouble when people are squeezed together in cracker boxes," he said.

"I meant anything unusual," Joseph explained.

"These are unusual times," said Saez. "The road has become heavy with different kind of people than maybe we've seen before. Impoverished migrants from as far away as Nicaragua. Starving Indians forced from their lands and then swept up like dust into refugee camps. Families ripped apart. Fathers forced to join the long march north. It's happened before, but never in such numbers."

"How do these people mix with the braceros who've been coming up for years?" asked Joseph. "Is there much friction between them?"

"Of course," Saez replied. "For a lot of reasons. Differences of language and culture for one. But more than that, these new migrants have become a threat to the Farm Workers Union. The union had finally gained some bargaining power after year's of hard and bloody fighting. They don't want to see it all go down the tubes. But these new migrants, the Mixtecs and the Quiche and the Misquitos, who often speak only their native tongues, have different values than the traditional braceros. Besides the language problem, they have different loyalties. Their ties are to their commune back home. They don't follow the same codes. And, worst of all, they're willing to live in conditions that most farm workers no longer accept..." He stopped. And then, looking directly into Joseph's eyes, he said, "You're interested in the Salvador Garcia case?"

Joseph nodded. "Let me get this straight. Are you saying the labor camp was divided into factions – Mexican and Indian?"

"It's not that simple," said Saez. "The migrant camp is more diverse. But it is divided along language lines. And the Indians tend to keep to themselves."

"How would you describe them generally. Would you say they're prone to violence?"

"It's dangerous to generalize. Especially in a place like this. But in my own experience the Indians from Central America tend to be a very gentle people. They don't get into many fights. Unless their honor is at stake."

"How far are they likely to go if their honor is at stake?" asked Joseph.

"How far are you?" Saez replied. "But if you're asking whether they've been socialized to our notions of crime and punishment, the answer probably would be no. Many of these Indians find themselves in a cultural limbo when they pass from their own world into ours. Sometimes nothing makes sense to them. A misunderstanding can become magnified to a point of no return."

"Is that what happened to Salvador Garcia?" Joseph felt the metal cup to see if the coffee was cool enough to drink. All the heat and dust had given him a parched throat.

"I didn't know Salvador," he said. "That incident happened before I arrived. But I can understand how a young Central American Indian, still innocent to the ways of the North, might find himself accused of murder without knowing what it meant."

Joseph took a sip of coffee. It reminded him of the boiled java he used to make on camping trips.

"I've heard talk about some strange incidents around here. Rumors of ritual sacrifices. That sort of thing."

Saez rubbed the wide brim of his nose and made a face, as if the question irritated him.

"Whenever you have aliens passing through a settled community, you hear rumors like those. In Eastern Europe they thought Christian blood was drunk by Jews..."

"But the Central American Indians did go in for ritual

sacrifice. As far a I know, Jews didn't drink much Christian blood. In fact, it probably was the other way around."

Saez shook his head. "Ritual sacrifice is a bogeyman, Radkin. It's just another way of separating us and them. When the rich go out on a hunt and kill a stag, ripping open its guts and offering the heart to one hunter and the hooves to another, we say it's all in the name of sport. We might find it peculiar, but we're not ready to send out a vigilante mob."

"Has a vigilante mob ever threatened the labor camp?" asked Joseph.

"The threat is there," he said. "A few days ago there was a fire. Clearly arson. The stink of gasoline was all over the place. There weren't any injuries, thank God, but several families were burnt out."

"What did the authorities have to say?"

Saez gave him a sarcastic glance. "They said that they'd look into it."

"Well, thanks for your help," said Joseph, standing up to go.

"No other questions?" asked Saez, looking almost disappointed.

"There is one other thing," he said. "I was wondering whether people from the labor camp are ever recruited to work in the sausage factory."

Saez stood up too. "If they are, it's news to me," he answered.

Chapter 27

ON THE WAY back to Ecstasy, he stopped by the river and sat on the bank. The crisp, blue rushing stream beckoned like a desert mirage. He leaned over and scooped up some of the water into his hand and put it to his mouth. The sweetness was invigorating.

The afternoon heat had cooled down a bit thanks to a passing cloud. Lying on the grassy bank, looking up at the sky, he began to think of Polly and the kids and felt an ache in his chest.

He closed his eyes and other images passed through his mind. Elizabeth with hair of blazing red, her skin so creamy white. The face of a boy, a young man, with dark complexion and darker eyes, his brown hands clutching bars of steel. A young woman dressed in black, her slim body pressed against a rock. And the smell of burning flesh...

He opened his eyes and realized he had lost all sense of time. Had he been asleep? he wondered. It had seemed like only a minute, but it was already turning to dusk.

Gabriella was waiting for him when he reached the Gazette, nervously pacing up and down.

"What happened to you?" she asked. "It's late!"

"Sorry," he said. "Something came up..."

She glanced at her watch. "I've arranged a meeting with Tippett. We haven't much time!"

"The translator who contacted Salvador's defense committee after the trial? How'd you get in touch with him?"

"He rang. Said he wanted to speak with Felix. He didn't know anything about the fire..."

"What did he say?"

"I got the impression that he feels his life's in danger. But he wouldn't speak with me. He didn't want to talk over the phone..."

"So you arranged a meeting?"

"I said you were a big-name reporter. That maybe you could help. He's anxious to talk to you – to us – but he wants it done his way..."

Joseph rubbed his eyes, wearily. "I should have talked to him myself," he said. "Don't ever make concessions for me..."

"Believe me," she said, "it was the only way. It was hard enough keeping him from hanging up on me..." She looked at him, hurt.

"OK," he said. "Forget it. What did you arrange?"

"We're supposed to meet him in about twenty minutes from now. He gave me instructions. It's about a thirty minute drive from here. He said he wouldn't wait for us..."

"He'll be there if he wants to talk," Joseph said, heading toward the door. "And he won't if he doesn't."

Chapter 28

"GO SOUTH ON the highway for five miles," she said, reading from her handwritten instructions. "Then keep your eye out for a farm road. Not the first, but the second one down. There's an old Burma Shave sign, he said. It's right after that."

The moon was bright. Otherwise they would have missed it. It was an old wooden sign which looked as if it had been there for centuries. The writing was half worn off. "Use Bum-S-ave," it read. And there was the ubiquitous face covered with foamy lather that he remembered seeing as a kid.

"Left at the next turning," she said.

The road he turned up wasn't paved and the mud holes were hell on the suspension. "You sure we shouldn't take the turning just after this one?"

"That's what he told me," Gabriella assured him after double checking her notes. "Another two hundred yards there should be two old oaks with a narrow drive between them. Pull into the drive and park."

"If we make it," he said. The road was getting bumpier. Clearly it hadn't been maintained for years. There might have been a farm up here, he thought, but not a farmer. At least not one who cared about his car.

"There!" she called out. "You passed it!"

"Those aren't oaks," he said. "They're maples."

"Of course they're oaks! Stop the car and back up!"

He did as she said.

"Where'd you learn your trees?" she asked. "In Brooklyn?"

"What's the difference?" he said, getting out. "A tree's a tree and a flower's a flower. Where to now?"

"Straight up the drive," she said, walking briskly in front of him.

For someone who was in strange territory, he thought, she was walking awfully fast. So maybe it wasn't so strange to her. After all, she knew an oak from a maple. But he knew the difference between smog and sea mist.

Pushing their way through a thicket of bramble, they found themselves in an overgrown garden at the rear of an old wooden farm house. From its derelict appearance it seemed to have been abandoned years ago and left to the mercy of the elements. Vines grew wildly over the facade, feeding constant moisture into the timber. The smell of damprot was everywhere.

"There's an old set of swings by the side of the porch," she said. "We're to wait over there."

"Why all the precautions?" he asked, as they fought their way through a tangled jungle of weeds. "It probably would have been safer to meet at the Holiday Inn down the highway." He kicked at a rusty watering can he had stumbled over, filling his shoe with oozing crud.

The swing set was just some corroded metal crossbars with two broken chains hanging down. It was several feet to the side of what once had been an enclosed sun porch. Left to moulder over the years, the frame of the enclosure had become encrusted with dirt and a myriad of cob webs.

"What now?" asked Joseph, feeling the wetness in his shoe creep up his sock. They were waiting by the swing set. He felt the cold rust of the corroded bar eat into his hand as he held on for support while standing on one leg to dump out the guck.

"We wait," she said. And then she looked around, nervously. "Christ! It's spooky here!"

He was wondering whether he had made another stupid mistake by stepping into something worse than what was in the rusty can, when he heard a voice call out:

"Gabriella Luna?"

"Yes," she replied, turning her head toward the direction of the voice. "Where are you?"

"I'm close enough," said the voice. "Is Mr. Radkin with you?"

"Yes," Joseph answered. "Why all the subterfuge? There's just the two of us here..."

"Look," said the voice, "this has to be done my way or not at all. Are we agreed?"

"We're agreed," said Gabriella.

"You're Miles Tippett?" asked Joseph.

"Yes," the voice replied.

"You're the translator who works for the Marsden Institute?"

"Yes. Except I no longer work for the institute..."

"Why are you hiding from us?" asked Joseph.

"I can't tell you that," said the voice.

"What can you tell us then?"

"Lighten up!" Gabriella whispered. "Don't push him!"

"I'll tell you some things. The rest you have to find out for yourself," the voice said.

"Why?" asked Joseph.

"I've got my reasons."

"What was your job with the foundation?" asked Joseph.

"I was doing research on Mayan hieroglyphs..."

"How long had you been working for them?"

"Several years."

"Are you a member of the New World Church?"

"No. I worked closely with them, however."

"Is there a relationship between Mundt, Grimes and the New World Church?"

"Not directly."

"Indirectly?"

"They have a business relationship."

"What kind of business?"

"I'm not sure. But I assume it has to do with Guatemala."

"Why do you assume that?"

"Because they were all there at the same time."

"When was that?"

"About ten years ago. Mundt ran a restaurant in Guatemala City. He called that one the Alfhem, too. Are you familiar with the reference?"

"Yes," aid Joseph.

"The Guatemalan Government thought it was a great joke. It became the hangout for anyone of importance."

"And Grimes?"

"Grimes was a small time dealer in Mayan artefacts."

"How did the New World Church fit into the pictures?"

"The Church was at its zenith at that time. They were heavily into missionary work in Guatemala. In 1982 a general who belonged to an evangelist group came to power, thanks to enormous financial aid from American fundamentalists. This gave the Protestant missionaries enormous influence..."

"To do what?"

"Whatever they wanted. The New World Church was in the forefront. They worked with messianic zeal. Their mission was to convert the last of the Mayan Indians to their own brand of evangelism."

"I'm still wondering how this relates to Mundt and Grimes," said Joseph.

"The missionaries from the New World Church were given posts in the various Indian townships, many of which were in regions that were so isolated that few white men had ever reached there..."

"Let me guess," said Joseph. "You were doing your Mayan research at one of these townships. Am I right?"

"Yes. I had been posted there with several missionaries. As I said, the Marsden Foundation worked closely with the Church. There were also several archaeologists who had been living with the Indians for a number of years. At the time we were posted they had just made a significant find. They had discovered a cave which contained numerous artefacts from classical Mayan times..."

"Did the Church have any relationship with the archaeologists?"

"The Church considered these archaeologists almost as big an enemy as the Marxist guerrillas."

"How come?"

"Because the archaeologists were trying to preserve the Mayan culture. The Church wanted to destroy it."

"So what you're saying is that there was conflict between the Church and the archaeologists. But the Church had the influence with the government. How did that work itself out?"

"By the archaeologists having their permits lifted. They were summarily removed from the country. The excavation site was given over to the Church."

"Can you give me the names of the archaeologists?"

"Just one. Harry Stanton. He's a professor at UCLA."

Joseph copied the name down in his notebook. "What did the Church do with the site?" he asked.

"They closed it up temporarily as it turned out. But I understand that something very important was found there."

"What?"

"I'm not sure."

"So how do Mundt and Grimes fit into the picture?"

"The military, of course, knew about the discovery. And the Alfhem was the center of all rumors and information, whether it was the latest CIA adventure or an archaeological find. Grimes and Mundt had already worked together doing some minor dealing. Grimes had the contacts with the art world, albeit the sleazier side. Mundt had the contacts with the military..."

"Are you saying they made a deal with the Church to dispose of the artefacts?"

"Not right away. But they must have negotiated something with them. The Church at that time was flush with funds, but several years later their base of financial support in the US started declining, especially after the exposure of all the fraud and malfeasance in the evangelist movement."

"But it's been a continuing relationship. And Mundt and Grimes moved up to Ecstasy."

"Yes. Because the Church's commune was based here."

"So why was that?" asked Joseph.

"You'll have to find that out for yourself," the voice replied.

"I'll need some more to go on," said Joseph. "Can't you give me anything else?"

"Something important was sent from Guatemala by diplomatic courier recently. There was a great deal of anticipation. Last month someone was sent to San Francisco to meet the shipment. At the same time, I was put under increased pressure to finish my translation into Mayan hieroglyphs..."

"What were you translating?" asked Joseph.

"A section of the New Testament from the Book of Revelations."

Joseph made another notation. Then he asked, "Why did you leave the foundation?"

"Because I didn't want to get mixed up with genocide," the voice said.

"I thought you said the Foundation was only involved in translating the Bible?"

"There's something terrible going on. I was just a small part of it. But it has to do with the annihilation of one of the most important civilizations that ever evolved on this planet. Their heritage is being destroyed and their history is being

114

forged..."

"I'm not sure I know what you're talking about," said Joseph.

"I can't tell you any more," said the voice. "But if you think about what I said, maybe you can figure it out. I understand you're a pretty clever reporter..."

Joseph wasn't sure what he thought of that comment. "What I can't figure out is why you're being so elusive. If you trust us enough to say what you did, why can't we speak face to face?"

"Like I said before, I have my reasons. That's all I can say for now. But it's an important story. Maybe the most important story you'll ever write..."

"How can I be certain anything you told me is true?" said Joseph. "I just can't accept a blind interview like this..."

"I wouldn't expect you to," said the voice. "I've given you as much as I can give. You'll have to take what I said and follow it up..." There was a moment of silence. Then the voice said, "Gabriella?"

"Yes?" she replied.

"I told you the interview would last precisely fifteen minutes. That time is up. I expect you to respect our agreement."

"Of course..." she replied.

"Wait a goddamn minute!" Joseph cut in. "I never made any agreement! I don't work like this!"

"Joseph!" Gabriella grabbed him by the arm. "I gave him my word and I brought you along on trust! I acted in good faith and I expect the same of you!" Through the darkness he could see her glaring at him a black cat with luminescent eyes.

"You've got to be kidding!" he said, pulling his arm away and moving swiftly in the direction of the porch. "We're not playing games, Gabriella. I can protect a source as well as anyone, but I don't like being made into a sucker!"

By the time he reached the back stairs, he could hear footsteps running through the interior of the house. He pulled at the handle of the rotten door and it came off in his hands. He pushed and the door fell crashing to the ground.

Moving swiftly over the debris, he made his way through the empty house, fighting his way though the darkness and the cobwebs. In front of him, he heard a door open and then slam shut.

He followed the sound, going through another large, empty room, tripping over missing floorboards, until he got to the front. He opened the door in time to see a figure running in the direction of a car. But in the darkness he could only see his silhouette.

Outside, the car had started up. Joseph watched it speed off down the road that ran along the frontage. Unlike the farm road that led to the back, and hidden from sight by the woods, this one was well-paved so the getaway was fast.

He took out his pad a made a note: "Car – black Honda Civic." Unfortunately, he didn't get the license number.

Chapter 29

HE GRABBED THE phone as soon as he got back to the Gazette and dialed the LA operator. There were three Stantons listed, first name Harry. The second try clicked. "You got me on the run," said Stanton. "I'm catching the night flight to Mexico City..."

"This will only take a minute," Joseph said, holding his pencil at the ready. "I understand you were on a dig in Guatemala back in the early 80's..."

"And before that I was in the Yucatan. What's this about?"

"I just spoke to someone who worked for the Marsden Institute during that time. He told me about some problems there with the New World Church..."

"Problems? I'll say! Those people are the scum of the

116

earth!"

"Yeah. I've heard that before. From a Catholic priest, if you can believe it..."

"I can believe it. Those crazy evangelists have as much to answer for as Diego de Laida did in his day..."

"Sorry," said Joseph, "the reference escapes me. Who's Diego de Laida?"

"A Franciscan friar. Embodied the spirit of the Inquisition. In 1594 he took it on himself to eradicate the Mayan religion and culture. Near his monastery in the Yucatan, a repository of ancient hieroglyphic books were discovered. De Laida had them burned. For any Mayan scholar, he's become history's arch villain. Jeremiah Cross comes in a close second..."

"The person I spoke with told me about a cave you discovered that contained some ancient Mayan artefacts. He said it was an important discovery..."

"All discoveries like that are important. This one was especially interesting."

"Why's that?"

"Because along with a good selection of pots there also were some things that would have helped us understand more about Mayan technology..."

"I don't understand," said Joseph. "You mean tools? Things like that?"

"Tools, yes. But the classical Mayas also manufactured their own paper. It was an elaborate process and they didn't make much. As far as we can tell, they only used it for their codices."

"'Codices'? What's that?"

"Plural of codex. They were hieroglyphic books the Mayas used in their ceremonies. De Laida thought they contained 'lies of the devil'. He had them all destroyed. All that he could find, that is. Up until last year, it was thought that only three remained. Now it's thought there were four. One of the things we found in the cave was a storehouse of supplies..."

"Like what?"

"Things like jars of vegetable substances they used for paint, natural gum for strengthening the pages and samples of the paper, itself. But we could only examine these things briefly before the government took away our permit ... look, I've got to go..."

"Just one thing more. Was there anything in that cave which would be exceptionally valuable to a collector?"

"The pots and a variety of other art objects. In today's market they'd bring in some money."

"A lot?"

"Depends on what you mean by that. A few thousand dollars is a lot of money to me. The art objects we found there were interesting, but not really top notch. The pots would be worth five or six hundred dollars each on the open market. But there's been so much looting going on that there aren't many Mayan treasures left. Now even second rate stuff costs a pretty penny from the unscrupulous scoundrels who deal in the cultural property trade..."

Joseph completed writing up his notes after Stanton had hung up. Then, looking up at Gabriella, who was still glaring at him from her perch on the couch, he asked, "Still pissed at me?"

"Yes!" she growled.

"Good!" He gave her a practised grin. "Then maybe you don't want to come..." He said that as he got up.

"Where?" Her eyes followed his movement, as he walked to the door.

"You know where," he said.

Chapter 30

HE DROVE THE short distance to the south side of town and then parked on a deserted street. "I hope you wore

118

sensible shoes," he said, turning to her as he slipped the keys out of the ignition.

"Why?" she asked, giving him a funny look.

"Because we're going to do a bit of hiking."

He had parked at the foot of Avenue C, where it met Third Street. Behind Third Street was a wooded hill covered with a dense growth of redwood and pine. Earlier, when they had driven past the sausage factory, Joseph had noticed that from those heights someone would have a good view of the factory loading dock while being camouflaged by the vegetation.

They approached the hill a safe distance away and climbed up about fifty feet before heading across the ridge. Finding a good observation point behind a stately redwood, they crouched down and waited.

The light from the moon illuminated the scene they were watching. It was being played out, Joseph supposed, as a consequence of Gabriella's finger in the sausage trick.

Two lorries were backed up to the loading dock of Mundt's sausage company. Several wooden crates were piled on the loading bay. A pair of burly men were carrying them from the warehouse out to the dock, while another two were loading them into the trucks.

"Must be heavy baggage judging from the size of those hunks doing the lifting," said Gabriella.

"Even if you're shipping out a quail's egg, you need twenty pounds of packing to make sure it didn't splatter. But one thing about sausages they're not likely to break."

They waited for what seemed like hours. Finally, Gabriella said, "It seems to me they're clearing out the place." She turned her face so the moonlight exposed the determined look in her eye. "This isn't doing us much good!"

"You have another suggestion?" he asked her.

"Damn right!" she said, getting up from her crouching position.

"Gabriella!" he hissed. But all he could do was watch as she disappeared into the shadows.

Chapter 31

WHAT SHE WAS up to wasn't clear until Joseph saw a silhouette of a slim figure edging its way along the side of the factory, around the corner from the loading bay. He kept one eye on her and another on the men carrying the crates, while trying to think of what he would do if she were caught.

The loading continued and Gabriella waited silently in the shadows, occasionally peeking around the corner to keep track of the men's progress.

Joseph pressed a button on his watch that lit up the dial and saw the seconds tick away. It was nearly three AM. By a quarter past the hour, one of the trucks closed its loading doors and drove away.

Now two men were left. They disappeared into the truck, probably to adjust the cargo. Considering the size of the load, it would take some time, he thought.

Then he saw her step out into the moonlight and look up in his direction. He came out from his hiding place and signalled to her by thrusting his arm like the starter of a race.

"Go!" he whispered loudly. She couldn't hear him of course. It came out of his mouth as a burst of anxious tension.

Like a cat, she leapt swiftly around the corner and then climbed silently onto the platform of the loading dock, on the blind side of the remaining truck. In another instant she had disappeared through the warehouse doors.

A moment later the two men came out of the truck. They went immediately inside the warehouse. Joseph slapped his forehead and cursed. Maybe there were more crates inside or maybe they were just doing some cleanup work. Whatever the reason, he hoped she heard them coming.

He lit the dial of his watch and checked the time. Ten

minutes later he checked the time again. At half past the hour the two men finally came out carrying another crate. They set it on the platform and began to discuss something intently. One of the men gesticulated anxiously with his hands and pointed to the crate. The other shrugged his shoulders. Then the first man took a hammer from a tool belt around his waist and hit the top of the crate on all four corners while the other went to lock the warehouse doors.

When the doors were locked and the nailing completed, the men loaded the last crate into the truck, climbed into the cab and drove off.

Running along the side of the hill, Joseph managed to keep the truck in view as it drove down the street. He saw it stop at the road that ran along the river. If they turned right, they would be headed toward the highway, Joseph thought. But they didn't. They made for the bridge, instead, crossing the river and heading down the small road, west. He watched them till they were out of sight. Then he ran back to the sausage factory.

Climbing onto the loading dock, he went over to the huge double doors. He tried them. They were securely locked.

"Gabriella!" he called out as he pounded his fists against the door. "Can you hear me?"

He put his ear to the door and listened.

"Gabriella!" he shouted again. Still there was no response.

Climbing back down to the pavement, he walked around the building, inspecting for windows. At the opposite end, he found one but it was too high for him to reach.

He bent down, picked up a stone and tossed it at the window.

"Gabriella!" he shouted.

Nothing.

He rubbed his chin, thought a minute and then decided to go back to the Gazette for a ladder.

Walking back to where he parked the car, he tried to picture the scene on the loading dock once again. The two men were arguing about something. Maybe they were debating what to do with her. Or, even worse, what to do with her body. He imagined her inside the create one of them had nailed shut white as a sheet and no longer breathing.

Twenty yards on, he saw his car. When he got a little closer, he could see someone was in it.

She was sitting in the driver's seat, smiling.

"You're OK," he laughed when he got up to the car. "I didn't think you had it in you. But you're OK!"

"You'd be surprised what I have in me," she replied, opening her purse. She took out some pieces of ceramics and laid them on the seat.

"Let me guess," he said, picking up one of the fragments and inspecting it. "A Mayan pot."

"Yes," she said. "From the classic period. Around fifteen hundred years old, I suspect."

"You opened up the crate," he said, staring at her and thinking to himself that the kid really had some guts. "How'd you do it?"

"There were some tools lying around on a bench. They'd obviously been warehousing a ton of artefacts there. I bet they had to work night and day to crate them."

"That whole warehouse space was taken up by artefacts?" he asked, marvelling at the enormity.

"No. Not all. There was something else..."

"Sausages?"

"Not sausages. Strawberries. Skads of them. And they were huge. The biggest I've ever seen."

"Any giant shortcake to go along with them?"

Ingnoring his attempt at humor, she asked, "Did you see where they were headed?"

"They crossed the Third Street bridge. Where does it lead?"

"Going west? To farming country..."

"You wouldn't use it to get to the coastal road, would you?"

"No. It's much faster to use the highway."

He turned and looked toward the river. The moon was brightening up the night again after having hidden behind a cloud. There was enough light on the horizon to see the distant mountains.

"They must be headed for the commune," said Gabriella.

Chapter 32

IT WAS JUST about four AM as they drove over the Third Street bridge. In another hour it would be light, he thought.

The early morning mist streaked across the windshield as he drove west toward the shadowy mountains. It gave the world a strange and eerie glint, bending the moonlight through a liquid filter.

It was a twenty minute trip through rolling woodlands before they came to the Valley of Heavenly Light which Gabriella said had been thusly named by Cross himself (or so the story went). The New World Church owned all the land for miles, she said.

As the reached the boundaries of the ranch, she pointed to the signs on a fence that ran off to eternity, warning, simply, that trespassers would be shot.

"Strong words for a Christian community," said Joseph, pulling up by the gate.

"They probably don't mean it," she said. "But when you've got this much land to fence, it's more cost effective than a barking dog..."

"Except a barking dog might bite," he said, driving the car onto the firm shoulder of the road and parking it out of sight, behind some bushes. They got out and walked over to the access road, closed off by an iron gate.

"This fence has a bite in it, too," she said, pointing out the topping of razor wire.

"Have you ever been here?" he asked her.

She shook her head.

"How about Felix or Elizabeth?"

"I don't know," she said.

The access road disappeared into a grove of redwood trees, rising from the ground like ghostly giants of the night. Beyond that, all was invisible.

"What now?" she asked.

"You didn't bring a wire-cutter with you, by any chance?" He looked at her as if it were a distinct possibility.

"Too cumbersome," she said. "You'd need a pretty big cutter to slice through chain that thick."

He put his hands into his trouser pockets, as if studying the situation. Too bad there wasn't a doorbell, he thought.

"What do you carry with you in the car?" she asked.

"Not much." He looked back to where the car was hidden. "Just stuff to change a tire."

"Why don't you get it?" she suggested, kicking the earth with the toe of her boot. "The ground here's pretty soft."

He went to the car and brought back the tire iron and a plastic bucket and shovel.

"What's that?" she asked, looking at the bucket and shovel.

"It belongs to the kids. Sand toys..." He looked down at the shovel. It was about six inches long. "Works great on the beach," he said.

Shaking her head, she took the tire iron from him and started digging into the soil at the foot of the fence. After she loosened the topsoil, Joseph got down on his knees and started digging out the chunks with the plastic shovel. Gabriella squatted opposite him and used the bucket as a scoop, cleaning the loosened dirt from what was quickly becoming an underpass for a small rodent, at least.

When they had gotten to hard ground again, Joseph took the tire iron and loosened some more dirt. Then, scooping out the pieces, they switched around again. Working this way, they soon had burrowed underneath the chain.

"Lousy job of fencing," he said, seeing that the metal jutted only half a foot underground.

"Don't complain," she said, lying down on hr back and wriggling her body into the channel they had constructed. She barely made it through. Standing up and brushing off the dirt, she said, "With your bulk, I think we'll need to dig a few more inches."

It didn't take long to finish the job. He squeezed underneath and then they went off into the darkness.

Chapter 33

THEY HAD WALKED for almost a quarter of a mile through woods and grassland before reaching any sign of human presence other than the road and a few fresh tire markings indicating recent traffic.

Then they found themselves passing through a cultivated field, neatly furrowed and carefully maintained. But there was something peculiar about it.

Gabriella was the first to realize. "I don't think I've ever seen vegetables like that," she said.

It wasn't the particular vegetables that struck Joseph, who didn't know a turnip from a parsnip. It was their size. They were magnificent. Tomatoes as big as red-eyed melons, corn stalks so high you'd need a ladder to climb them, berries like the ripe, juicy schnozz on a slaphappy drunk.

Kneeling down, Gabriella pulled up a potato plant and brushed off the dirt which clung to the tuber. Then, taking a knife from her all-purpose bag, she cut out a chunk and held it up to the feint light of the morning sun.

"Look," she said. "It's purple."

"So what?" he said. "Maybe all potatoes look like that

before they're ripe..."

"They don't," she said. "These are special."

"I'm a pasta man, myself," he said, shrugging his shoulders.

"I've only read about them," she said. "I know they found the seeds..."

"What are you talking about?" he asked. "You want to let me in on it?"

"I don't know about the other stuff, but the purple potatoes are from Guatemala. Several years ago they found some isolated tribes, ancestors of the Maya, still growing them. I knew some agronomists in Southern California were trying to cultivate the seeds, but they were having trouble figuring out the proper way to grow them. They didn't really have the know-how..."

"Well, these people certainly do," he said, glancing over at a sunflower that was nearly seven feet high. "We're in the land of giant fruits and vegetables."

Gabriella had gone over to the strawberry patch. "Look at the size of these things," she said, pulling one of the berries from its stem and holding it up for inspection. The huge, ripe fruit was covered in glistening dew. "Just like the ones in the warehouse," she said.

"I wonder what the rabbits are like here," he said, glancing nervously around.

"Never mind about the rabbits..." Her voice had suddenly grown quiet. She reached for his hand.

Joseph followed her line of sight out toward the horizon and then realized what her problem was. In the distance, the field sloped up. On the crest of the incline there was a group of men, standing like shadows, watching them.

"You got any suggestions now?" she asked.

"No, but we might as well make contact," he said, standing out in the open and waving at the figures in the distance.

He had noticed that one of them was pointing at him with a stick before he heard the sound. It was like a whistle. And instant later the corn stalk next to him exploded, splattering atomized vegetable flesh all over.

It smelled a little like popcorn – that was the crazy thought which leapt into his head as he threw himself to the ground. There was a moment's delay before the adrenaline started pumping through his bloodstream. Then he looked around, frantically trying to size up the situation. He saw Gabriella was on her belly, too. On their right was the woods. To their left, the fields went on as far as he could see. Behind them was the road, but it provided no cover. He pulled at her hand and, staying low, camouflaged by the giant vegetables, they took off toward the shelter of the forest.

Chapter 34

THERE WAS A primeval feel about the ferns and the moss and the damp mulch under their feet. Even in the dawning light the place was dark, with just soft traces of haze filtering through the denseness of the trees.

They walked for what seemed like hours. But when he pressed the luminescent dial of his watch, he saw it was only a quarter past six. "The problem is the deeper we go, the longer we walk, the more likely it is that we're thoroughly lost," she complained.

"I thought you knew trees," he said.

"I know the genre. I don't know them personally – not on a first name basis," she said, stopping to sit down on a mossy log.

The place was filled with strange sounds strange, at least, to him. In the darkness of the woods, the nocturnal creatures were still awake. Above them, a pair of glowing eyes stared down, while the forest bristled with the echo of a hooting owl.

"Look," he said, "in case we get separated and you find

your way out, I keep a spare key under the driver's seat in a magnetic box." He took his notebook from his jacket pocket, scribbled something down and then ripped the page out. "Here's the number of the wire service I work for. Ask for Tarzan. Tell him what's going on. He'll know what to do..."

"I'd rather we stick together," she said, grabbing hold of his hand and giving it a squeeze. Somehow that made his stomach feel even more queasy.

"We need to find the way back to the road," she said.

"The road is the last place we want to be if they've got a policy of shooting first and asking afterwards," he replied.

"I don't mean to walk down it. But as long as we can keep it in sight, we know which direction we're headed. Right now, we're probably going in circles." She looked up toward the tops of the trees. "The vegetation's so dense here, it's hard to see the sky..."

"It's too late to start wishing on stars," he said.

"I mean for navigation." She got up and went over to one of the trees and ran her fingers over the bark.

"Making friends?" he asked, watching her. He thought she looked more at home here than she did at the Gazette.

"Feeling the moss. You can sometimes tell direction by which side of the tree the moss grows on. The forest is a living organism, a triumph of symbiosis. If you understand it, you can find your way through..."

"To me a forest is a place to have a shady picnic," he said. "If you don't go too deep and you're careful where you step..."

She stopped his chatter by putting a finger to her lips and looking into the distance.

"What?" he asked, looking at her curiously.

"I thought I heard something."

"Something? With all that hooting and howling?"

"It sounded like a twig cracking."

"I just scratched my foot. Maybe I cracked it."

"No. The sound came from someplace else..."

128

He glanced around. Twenty feet on, the forest retreated into darkness. Anything could be out there, he thought. Including a headless horseman. He took out his pack of cigarettes, pulled one out and lit up.

"Don't be a fool!" she hissed.

He looked over at her. "Who are you? Smoky-the-Bear?"

Her face was tense. "You might as well wear a beeper!" she said. "Or shine a flashlight in the air!"

She went over to the next tree, to feel it up too, he guessed. "Strange how people get their kicks when they've gone back to hunt and gather," he said, watching her in wonder.

"What do you suggest?" she asked.

"Have another cigarette. Wait another hour till it gets lighter. Then follow the trail of bread crumbs I left..."

"It'll be dark here for a long time," she said, going to the next tree down. "This forest is pretty dense..."

Her voice was getting more distant as she faded further into the woods. "This way is east, I'm sure of it..."

He got up and stubbed his cigarette out. Looking around, he could no longer see her. "Gabriella?" he called out.

"I'm over here" The voice was distant. It echoed like the hooting of the owl.

He took a few tentative steps in the direction he thought she had gone. "Gabriella?"

"Over here..."

Her voice was even more distant now.

He took another step and that's when it happened. He heard a snap and then something grabbed his leg. Suddenly his body was ripped from the ground and he was flung into the air. In that moment before the rush of terror, when he caught his breath and once again opened his eyes, he realized he was swinging from a tree limb.

Chapter 35

HE WAS BARELY conscious when they cut him down and carted him off, tied to a deerskin litter. Every so often a burst of morning light came through the thick arboreal canopy, blinding him in brightness. Then, after a moment, the sky closed up, plunging him into haze again, and the world once more became a shadowy blur.

There was a moment when he thought he saw a butterfly dance before his eyes, its delicate wings softly cutting through the air, hovering before him, painting the muted rays with its magnificent hues. But that might have been the ghost of an image locked in his retinal memory. For the dominant sight was the ground and the tan heel and muscular thigh of a barefoot man who carried the litter he was tied onto from the front.

That's what he saw. What he heard was the rhythmic patter of the bearers as they moved swiftly over the ground as smooth as antelopes, and the sound of ferns brushing against their skin.

And then the world lit up. They were out of the woods. The air was crystal clear. The sky was brilliant blue. He felt the cold mist of morning on his face.

He saw the patterns of the clouds staring down at him from the heavens. He felt the movement pick up. The patter of the feet became a thud. The soil had changed. No longer the softness of the mulch but the hardness of the rock. He smelled the odor of fire and cooking meat.

The pace of the bearers picked up. The rhythm became more intense. Then all at once they stopped. He heard the opening of a door and he was brought inside a hut.

He felt himself being lowered to the ground. He heard the bearers run off, leaving him tied securely to the litter.

The door closed and suddenly it grew dark.

He was alone. He didn't know where. He felt something slither up his leg. It could have been a snake. It could have been a tarantula or a scorpion. He didn't know what it was but as it moved slowly toward his thigh, he opened his eyes as wide as they could open and shouted at the top of his lungs, "Help! Goddamn it! Help!"

"Joseph? Is that you?" a voice whispered.

"Gabriella? There's something crawling up my leg!"

"Ants," she said. "The place is full of them."

"It's bigger than an ant!" he said. He wriggled in his bindings, but they were securely tied.

"Can you move at all?" she asked. "Try shifting your weight back and forth..."

He tried what she said and found that by rolling his body one way and then the other, he could force the stretcher to skip, little by little, across the dirt floor.

"Keep talking," he said to her. "I'll try to move in your direction..."

She did just that, telling him about her capture soon after Joseph had been caught in the sling trap. She had heard a sound like a whistle and then had felt something prick her skin. A dart, she suspected. It probably contained some sort of tranquillizer that acted on her central nervous system, because, within moments she felt her legs give way and she collapsed to the ground. She lay there, helpless, until they came and scooped her up. It was only now that she felt able to move her limbs.

The sound of her voice came closer as he forced the litter to slide, one painful inch at a time, across the floor. Until he felt himself bump against something soft.

"Is that you?" he asked.

"Yes," she said. "Slide down until we're hand to hand."

He worked his way down as she, simultaneously, tried to work her way up. Then he felt the warmth of her fingers.

"Hi," he said. "How are you?"

131

"Terrified!" she exclaimed. "How about yourself?"

"I've been better. Can you get a grip on the knot?"

"I'm trying. I just don't seem to have any strength!"

"Don't you have a knife in your purse?" he asked.

"Yes, but I don't know where my purse is."

"Listen," he said, "I'll move down a little more. See if you can reach inside the pocket of my jacket..."

"You have a knife?"

"No, but I have a lighter."

He manoeuvred himself into position and they rolled together, until they were mouth to mouth and he could feel and smell and taste her as she rummaged through his pockets for his Ronson.

"Found it!" she whispered. "What now?"

"Try lighting it," he said.

"But I'll roast you alive!"

"I don't think so. I've tried burning rope before. It smoulders rather than catch on fire. I've tried it in the barbecue. It's absolutely useless as a starter..." Then, thinking about the one time he did throw in a piece that lit, he said, "However, I'm open to other suggestions..."

"I'll give it a shot," she said. "Anyway, my mouth's close enough to blow out the flame..."

She lit him up. He closed his eyes and gritted his teeth. He could smell the burning hemp. It was a strong odor. Strong enough to mask the smell of roasting flesh.

"I just can't do it!" she said after blowing the flame out. "How about if I try chewing the damn thing off?"

"Try anything you like!" he said, feeling a cold sweat come over his body while whatever-it-was crawled further up his leg.

She had jaws of steel, he thought, as she ripped and pulled at his binds. he felt her moist breath on his skin, cooling his burns.

"Try pulling your hands apart!" she whispered.

Putting every ounce of strength into it, he managed to

loosen the ropes. Now grabbing a sagging loop with her jaws, she pulled again and suddenly his hands were free.

Quickly, he undid the other binds and jumped up. He pulled off his trousers and grabbed the slithering thing he couldn't see and threw it across the enclosure. Then, fastening his trousers once more, he knelt down and undid her bonds as she lit the Ronson to guide him.

"Where the hell are we?" he asked as he brushed himself off.

"I have no idea," she said.

He lit the Ronson again and walked slowly across the room as the light from the flame cast huge, distorted shadows on the walls of mud.

"Look there!" He pointed to a set of wooden shutters. "I'll lift you up. See if you can open them."

Making his arms into a sling, he gave her a boost high enough to get hold of the latch which secured the two wooden shutters together. She forced it loose. Then pulling the shutters open just a crack, she peered out.

"What do you see?" she asked.

"We're in some sort of village," she said. "Whitewashed adobe huts, dirt paths, small groups of people – Indians gathered around..."

"Indians?"

"Central American, judging by their costume. From the colors and design, I'd say they're Guatemalan..."

Suddenly the door burst open and the room was filled with light. Lowering Gabriella, Joseph turned in the direction of the bright beam of sun. He found it too intense to look at directly. Squinting his eyes he was able to make out the shimmering image of three men standing in the open doorway. The taller of the figures stepped forward.

"Welcome to the New World Commune," he said. "My name is Jeremiah Cross..."

Chapter 36

IT WAS A timeless world they had been transported to, thought Joseph, as the entourage walked along the muddy road which led through the Indian village. He had never been to Central America, but, even so, he would have bet that the reconstruction was perfect in almost every respect. It had that look of veracity, of truth. Like a well researched movie set.

But one thing struck him. He didn't know – maybe the Indians in Guatemala did things like that. Yet everyone he saw men, women, children, babies they all wore a silver crucifix around their neck.

Jeremiah Cross had the youthful presence of a middle-aged actor on amphetamines, sporting a long face and flowing hair that went well with his athletic figure. But it was his eyes that Joseph found most intriguing. They were sunk in his head like dime store gems encrusted in a ten penny crown; their limpid look highlighted by a heavy layer of mascara.

"Who are they!" asked Joseph, referring to the groups of Indians they passed.

"They are the chosen ones," Cross replied. "The ones who have been sent here by our ministry to learn the True Way of God..."

"Couldn't they learn it back home?" asked Gabriella. The tone of her voice made her feelings about that quite clear to Joseph, at least.

"The New World is at hand," replied Cross, matter-of-factly. "The Final Day of Judgement is upon us. They've joined us here so they could be free of temptation. When they're ready, they'll go back carrying the True World with them."

Joseph looked at the gentle faces of the brown-skinned people they passed and wondered what lay before them.

"They can be like children," Cross went on, smiling benevolently at the small clusters, as if responding to their quiet look of obedience. "But like children, they can resort to their pagan ways. It takes much time and patience before our teaching is firmly absorbed..."

"It wasn't these people who shot at us when we were in the fields," Joseph said, walking swiftly to keep pace with the man who claimed to be their prophet and their teacher.

"We've had our share of trouble with intruders," said Cross. "Our policy on trespass is strictly enforced."

"To the point of murder?" asked Joseph.

Cross stopped the procession and fixed Joseph with a stare that gave him a good opportunity to see the usefulness of painted eyes. "I believe you're still alive," he said.

It was just an opinion. As for Joseph, he wasn't too sure what he thought about the state of his mortality right then.

The path they were on led to a central plaza, dominated by a large, rectangular building with cathedral-like windows and a monumental crucifix. Facing it, on the other side of the plaza was another, smaller building. The doors to the smaller building were being guarded by two young, fair-haired disciples. A sign over the door read, "New World Education Project."

"What's in there?" asked Joseph, pointing back to the smaller building, opposite, as Cross led the way to the cathedral.

"That's where the word of God is being transmitted."

A radio station? Joseph wondered. Quickly glancing around, he saw no transmission aerials from that building though there was a satellite dish on the roof of the annex extending out from the cathedral.

It was the annex they entered – a large reception room, with panoramic photos of mountains and seascapes.

As several of the disciples ushered Gabriella off to a

135

separate waiting area, Cross directed Joseph to a door which was being guarded by another hollow-eyed ex-druggy, Joseph thought, and escorted him through.

The room was tiny just large enough for them and maybe a mouse, if the mouse held its breath. Cross pressed a button on the wall and, before Joseph had a chance to catch onto where he was, the room descended, leaving his stomach somewhere above.

Bottom was twenty feet below. When they arrived, two seconds later, they came into a hallway with doors on either side, each bearing notice of something administrative "Accounts", "Purchasing", "Publicity", "Personnel". Walking quickly down the hall, Joseph felt the bright, fluorescent lights and whitewashed walls jangle his nerves. They gave the place that same efficient and mind-numbing atmosphere that corporations around the world manage so well, he thought.

At the end of the hall was a door with a sign which read "Operations". Cross opened the door and led Joseph inside.

It was a large room with a huge map of Central America covering an entire wall. The map was dotted with colorful pins and overlays bearing numbers and letters which meant nothing to him though, he thought, they were probably codes of some sort.

The place was thick with electronic gear – computer terminals, closed-circuit TV screens, copiers, shredders and the ubiquitous fax machines. All this was being tended by a corps of scrubbed-down women dressed in white.

Cross continued through the work center, past desks stacked high with form-fed listing paper and data tapes, toward a door marked "Central Planning" and a sign that read "Only Authorized Personnel".

It was dark inside the room where Cross had led him. Once inside, with the door closed behind them, Cross reached over and turned on the light.

The first thing Joseph thought when he looked around was that maybe he had ended up in the private study of an exclusive men's club. The room was quiet, smelled of musk and was comfortably leathered. Over the fireplace was the head of an elk.

Cross pointed to an easy chair. "Have a seat," he told Joseph.

Joseph did as instructed, while Cross went over to a well-stocked liquor cabinet. "What's your poison?" he asked. "We've got most anything you'd want Jim Beam, Canadian Club, Seagrams..." He took a bottle of white liquor and held it out. "This one's made of fermented cactus."

"I'll stick to grain, if you don't mind," said Joseph. "You have any Scottish stuff?"

"Used to be my favorite too," said Cross, pulling out a bottle of Glenfiddich and pouring a glassful. "Don't want to ruin it with ice, do you?" he asked.

"You're on the wagon, I take it," said Joseph, watching Cross open up a bottle of mineral water for himself.

"Haven't touched alcohol in twenty years," said Cross, bringing over the drinks and placing them down next to a folder lying on a round, inlaid wooden table. The table rested between two easy chairs, one of which was occupied by Joseph. Cross sat himself in the other and picked up the folder.

The folder contained some computer data sheets which Cross quickly skimmed through. Then, looking back at Joseph, he said, "You've been around, I see. Worked on quite a few newspapers and magazines, but didn't last long on any of them."

Joseph took a drink of the Glenfiddich and glanced over the top of the glass at the man across from him. "I like to keep my options open," he replied.

Cross pulled out a Xeroxed sheet from the folder and scanned it. "You write good copy though. Clear, concise, straight to the point..."

"Glad you appreciate it," said Joseph. He was always in the mood to accept complements. Especially if it was backed up by good whisky.

"Seems to me you have problems, Mr Radkin," said Cross, putting the sheets of paper back into the file and staring at him with magnetic eyes. "Wife, two children, mortgage payments, no pension funds. What are you going to do when your kids reach college age? Have you thought of that? A good university runs ten to twenty grand a year. Multiply that by two and what have you got?"

A headache, Joseph thought. But what he said was, "You're not offering me a job, by any chance, are you?"

"There's always room in our organization for someone with your skills," said Cross.

Joseph scratched the side of his head. He was expecting anything but a career opportunity. "I suppose I should say, right off, that I put religion above castor oil and enemas on my list of things to stay away from."

Cross smiled as wide as any used-car salesman and showed his gleaming teeth. "Don't write it off," he said. "Religion is a business, like anything else. You don't have to believe – not immediately, anyhow. Take me, for instance. I started as a property salesman. Made good money when the boom was on. Little less when the market went down. I had all the possessions I wanted, but no job satisfaction. I was rich and unhappy. Then I took to drink and started my descent into hell..."

"And afterwards you found God," said Joseph. "I hope you don't mind me cutting you off, but I read the book and saw the film..."

"You read it wrong then. God was the last thing I was looking for. He found me, I didn't find Him. He saw my troubled soul was up for grabs. And he made me an offer..."

"One you couldn't refuse, I take it."

"Oh, I could have refused," said Cross. "But I would have been a fool if I did. What he offered was everlasting life and salvation. Better than a Maseratti, any day! Wouldn't you agree?"

"I guess," said Joseph. "It really depends on the age of

the car."

"What if He offered you everlasting life, salvation and a Maseratti?" asked Cross, winking as if this was a little shared conspiracy.

"You mean sort of like a three for one sale?"

"Something like that, yes."

"Then I'd say you ought to check it out with Consumer's Union," said Joseph. "Polly always does..."

"Polly?"

"My wife."

"Perhaps you should think of her and the kids more often."

"Maybe I should," he said. He meant it at that.

Cross stood up, bursting with energy, like a coach of a college football team. "So what do you say, Radkin? I'll start you off at thirty grand a year, company car, good pension. If you play your cards right, within a year you'll be making fifty thousand, free tuition to a good private school for your kids and a lovely house for you wife."

"Where?"

"El Salvador."

"Is that where you sent that other reporter who was doing a story on you? McLean that's his name, wasn't it?"

"He's in Costa Rica and doing quite nicely."

"How about my friend the one you're keeping upstairs?"

"The woman who calls herself Gabriella Luna? Just that we couldn't find any data on her. Not under that name, anyhow. No ID in her purse no driver's license, credit cards or even social security number. I think she's trouble, Radkin..."

"Then what are you planning to do with her?" asked Joseph.

Cross shrugged his shoulders. "That's up to you."

"I don't think I could really work for the CIA," said Joseph. "And when it got right down to it, I don't think they'd like it much either."

"How about working for your own salvation, then?"

139

Joseph got up from his chair. "By dealing in stolen arte-facts?"

Cross' massacred eyes seemed to darken. "Perhaps I judged you wrong..."

"Maybe you have," Joseph said. "Am I free to go?"

"That's not up to me," said Cross. "Your future's in the hands of Christ and the brethren."

Chapter 37

HE WAS ESCORTED to the chapel by one of the brethren who might not have believed in Darwin but who, Joseph thought, was about as close to ape as one could get without craving bananas.

The chapel was more of a cathedral with high, vaulted ceiling and magnificent light which poured in through the colored glass. The classical effect was broken, however, by the brightly decorated banners hanging from the walls which read "PRAISE BE TO JESUS!", "GET READY FOR JUDGE-MENT DAY!", and "ONWARD TOWARD THE MILLEN-NIUM!"

The chapel was filled with young, clean-cut kids who watched his entrance with a combination of awe and amuse-ment. Joseph felt as if he had come to the main attraction of a circus sideshow only to find that he was it.

He was led to a little area against the wall which was set apart both from the congregation and the pulpit. If this wasn't a church, one could have seen it as a courtroom and the nook where he was taken as the dock.

Gabriella was already there, guarded by a Neanderthal who might have been his ape's twin brother.

"Where were you?" she asked, as he came up to her, giv-ing her hand a squeeze of reassurance.

"Having a job interview," he said.

At that moment a surge of electricity seemed to jolt through the room and a hush came over the assemblage as Cross suddenly appeared at the pulpit.

"Brethren!" he began, lifting his arms above his head in a gesture toward Heaven. "Today, God has once again decided, in his infinite wisdom, to test our strength, our fortitude and our everlasting faith by allowing the servants of Satan to enter our fold..."

Standing behind the table, which, he supposed, was reserved for the accused, Joseph whispered into Gabriella's ear "I think he means us..."

Cross thundered on: "They serve the Prince of Darkness by casting doubt. And by casting doubt, they sow the seeds of Despair. For Doubt is the Devil's Poisonous Fruit. It fills our head with Evil Thoughts and our Heart with Sinful Desire..."

"Amen!" shouted the assemblage.

"The devil comes to us in many forms. We know him well when he seeks us out in tablets and in drink. But the Devil has many disguises..."

The room again echoed with cries of assent.

"Today he may come as Sin. Tomorrow, disguised as Reason. He whittles slowly at our Faith. He waits for us to lose our guard. And then..."

Cross slammed his fist on the pulpit making a mighty, crashing sound. He pointed a finger toward the dock: "Brethren! Look ye upon the face of Evil!"

"He does mean us," said Gabriella, looking worriedly at Joseph. "Got any ideas?"

"No," replied Joseph, "but he does. And I don't particularly want to wait around to hear what he proposes..."

Cross's finger trembled with great effect. "Look ye upon Satan!"

The assemblage turned en mass to stare at Joseph and Gabriella. It was a moment when the world seemed to stop.

"If it's Hell Fire they want," Joseph whispered, "let's give it to them!"

141

And, he leapt up on the table making a practised face he used to terrify his children by forcing the whites of his eyes to stick out and pulling his hair so it stood on end. "Behold sinful Earthling creatures!" he shouted at the top of his lungs, "I am Vishnu!"

The assemblage, suddenly fearful at what might be unleashed upon them by this terrible apparition, shrank back in horror.

"I am the creator and destroyer of all worlds!" Joseph shouted, striking his Ronson and setting light to the huge banner hanging overhead which proclaimed, "THE NEW WORLD IS OURS!"

The draught from the doorway was just right. The fire quickly rose in a great ball of flame while Joseph, grabbing Gabriella's hand, ran out the side exit, leaving the brethren sobbing and shrieking in a state of mass confusion.

Running from the cathedral, they saw the fair-haired guards at the smaller building next door come toward them.

"Fire!" Joseph shouted, pointing to smoke now pouring through the chapel door. "People trapped! They need help!"

As the guards rushed up the stairs, Joseph ran into the smaller building marked "New World Education Project". Gabriella followed close behind him.

The Indians stopped and looked up, their stoic faces hardly betraying any sign of emotion. They stopped only for a moment, however. An instant later they had set to work again.

Over one wall was taped an enormous drawing a series of hieroglyphs. Underneath, a group of artisans were copying the intricate design onto ancient-looking paper.

Further down, other workers were grinding materials onto pigments and processing strange-looking vegetation into dye. Still others were using the dyes and pigments, meticulously, on ceramic pots.

"Amazing!" said Gabriella, absorbing the surroundings with a certain professional appreciation.

"Let's not stand and gawk!" said Joseph, grabbing her hand again and running toward an exit on the far side of the room.

The exit led to a back alley which ran between the building and a row of adobe huts. One way led to the central square. Joseph, still holding onto Gabriella's hand, hurried in the opposite direction.

At the end of the alley was a parking area where the two trucks they had seen leaving Mundt's sausage factory were parked.

Joseph ran up to the closest truck and opened one of the doors. "Quick! Climb inside!" he called out.

Gabriella leapt up onto the running board, looked inside and then, glanced back at Joseph. "No keys!" she shouted.

Joseph hurriedly scanned the surroundings. There was a little hut some thirty yards away with a sign that read, "Motor Pool." A large man was standing at the window staring at them curiously.

"Come on," Joseph shouted, helping her down. He pointed to the hut. "The keys are probably in there."

As they ran over, the bulky man stepped out of the hut and folded his arms.

"You got the keys to that rig?" Joseph asked.

"What for?" asked the man.

"Cross asked us to get them," said Gabriella, smiling sweetly.

"Keep your distance, Lady of Lust!" hissed the man.

"That really pisses me off!" Gabriella said, angrily, kicking him in the groin.

As the bulky man doubled over in pain, Joseph scurried into the hut and grabbed every set of keys he saw hanging from the wooden pegs.

"Come on!" he shouted, racing back to the truck and pulling her up after jumping in, himself.

By this time, however, a group of the brethren were advancing, shaking their fists high in the air and shouting,

"Death to Satan!"

Joseph furiously tried several different keys in the ignition. Each one failed to turn. Gabriella gave him a frantic nudge. "Here they come!" she shouted.

He looked up and saw a pose of men carrying shotguns headed down the alley toward them. Looking down at the keys, he groaned, "I can't find one to fit!"

"Just slam one in and turn it!" she shouted.

Suddenly, a shot rang out. The force of the blast threw her against him, as the windscreen shattered into tiny pellets.

"Maybe God's on their side after all," he said, brushing the bits of glass from his hair.

"Like hell!" she said and she took her shoe and pounded it against the key stuck halfway in the ignition.

He tried it and it turned.

"Drive!" she yelled, as another blast ricocheted behind them.

He stamped his foot on the accelerator and thrusting the old transmission into gear, the truck lurched forward, scattering the screaming mob.

They made for the road and were already headed for the gate when Gabriella looked back and saw a car in hot pursuit.

"Step on it!" she hollered.

"I've got the peddle to the metal!" he shouted back. "Anyway, they can't pass us on this one lane road!"

"Well, he's going to try!" said Gabriella.

Joseph looked behind him and saw a blue sedan trying to edge around his right. A shotgun blast rang out and he could feel the explosion of a tire.

At that moment, he veered to the left and felt his tire lurch into a rut. Clutching the wheel with all his might, he forced it back onto the road and with another quick movement made the truck veer toward the right just as the blue sedan tried to pass.

He felt the crash but they felt it more, he bet. The blue sedan swerved off the road, running down the embankment into he fields.

"That's one," he said, licking his finger and making a mark on the dashboard.

"Yeah," said Gabriella, sticking her head out the window. "But there's another..."

"Gate coming up!" he said.

"And it's locked!" she reminded him.

"We can't worry about that now!" he shouted. "Hold on!"

The truck smashed through the gate. He slammed on the brake and the truck spun around ninety degrees and stalled out.

"Jesus Christ!" she shouted. "They're coming fast!"

"Get out!" he yelled. "My car's parked across the road and we're blocking their exit!"

Sure enough, the truck was positioned so no one could get out the gate. Joseph reached back and grabbed a couple of pots as Gabriella jumped from the cab and ran over to the MG, waiting patiently like a horse at tether.

Chapter 38

THERE WAS ONLY one sanctuary he knew within easy driving distance and he went to it. When he got there, he brought the MG screeching to a halt.

Morning services had just been completed and Kinsolving was in the refuge making tea for some of his Spanish-speaking parishioners when Joseph and Gabriella burst in. He led them into an adjoining room so they could speak privately with him.

After patiently hearing them spill their guts out bolstered by years at the confessional, Joseph guessed, Kinsolving fixed up several beds in the dormitory and told them to get some sleep. It was an offer that both of them readily accepted.

Chapter 39

THE FIRST THING he saw when he woke up that afternoon was a crucifix hanging on the wall. But, unlike the one he saw the night before which glared at him as if he should have been nailed up there along side of it, this Christ, at least, looked forgiving, smiling down serenely as if to say, "Look, don't worry. Just say a few 'Hail Marys and we'll forget about it."

There was a smell of broiling bacon and fresh coffee coming from the refectory as he stumbled his way in. Gabriella was sitting at a table mopping up the remains of a fried egg with a hunk of bread. Kinsolving was bringing in a fresh pot of brew. He noticed Joseph and smiled in a motherly way, showing off his ragged choppers in the bargain. Joseph found himself wondering what kind of dental plan the church had for its employees. In his way of thinking, it probably was as good a way to choose your religion as any.

"We were just discussing new vegetables and old crockery," Kinsolving said. "What can I bring you to eat?"

That was better than his mother, thought Joseph. She would have just pointed to the kitchen.

"Coffee will be fine," Joseph replied, sitting down across from Gabriella. "How are you?" he asked, looking over at her.

Shrugging, she mopped up the last of her egg.

Kinsolving poured some coffee and handed it around. "I've been making some calls this morning, seeing what I could dig up..."

Joseph took the coffee, gratefully. It probably was instant, he thought, and he hated instant. But he wasn't about to make a fuss. "Who'd you call?" he asked.

"I have some contacts in the Governor's office. They've

146

been interested in the New World people for some time..."

"But they're not prepared to do anything," said Gabriella, looking grim.

"I didn't really say that," Kinsolving corrected. "What I said was they don't feel they can move in on them too fast."

"Too fast?" Gabriella looked at Joseph and let out a laugh.

"That's not me talking," Kinsolving was quick to assure her.

"What kind of investigation has been going on?" asked Joseph.

"Tax audits, questions concerning health and safety codes, zoning regulations things like that."

"Nothing to really hang them on, I bet."

Kinsolving shook his head. "They've got friends in very high places."

"How about the link with Mundt and Grimes?" asked Gabriella.

"That, of course, would be the key. But there's no real evidence, is there?" Kinsolving took a sip of his coffee and looked at each of them in turn.

"We've actually got quite a lot," Gabriella objected. "We know Mundt, Grimes and Cross were participating in a forged antiquities ring..." She looked over at Joseph. "Those pots we saw being painted at the New World Commune – they were the same as the ones we found in Mundt's warehouse."

"I'm not saying we don't have the basis for a whole range of crimes – fraud, theft, conspiracy and so on but I'm afraid that in order for us to get the immediate assistance of the State or Federal agencies, we need a smoking gun..." Kinsolving said, looking apologetic. "Otherwise, it's left in the category of 'ongoing investigations.'"

"There were plenty of smoking guns last night," Joseph reminded him.

"Ah, yes..." Kinsolving nodded. Then making another expression of regret, he said, "But you were trespassing. And the land was signposted. According to the letter of the law they were within their rights. In fact, they could easily press charges against the two of you. Stealing a truck is considered grand theft..."

Gabriella looked shocked. "You think they would?"

"They might," Kinsolving said.

"They won't," Joseph disagreed. "It would be opening up a can of worms for them."

"You're probably right" said Kinsolving. "But don't sell these people short. They've got a lot to protect."

"I don't sell them short at all," Joseph replied. "They're capable of anything except bringing us to court."

"Well, I wouldn't argue the point with you," said Kinsolving. "All I know is that the two of you have somehow managed to start a timebomb ticking. And nobody knows when it's set to go off."

Joseph took a cigarette from his pocket and lit up. "Look" he said, "Things happened. I'm not sure how, but they happened. And, in the process, a lot of crap's come rising up..." He glanced at Kinsolving.

"I wouldn't object to the substance of that remark," Kinsolving assured him.

"Anyway," Joseph continued, looking at Gabriella, "Elizabeth warned me there were a lot of layers to life around here."

"What are you getting at?" she asked him.

"I don't know. Nothing maybe..."

"Aren't you interested in the connections?"

"I'm always interested in connections," he replied. "I'm also interested in finding out what happened to the Mannings..."

"But there must be a link between the fire that killed them and everything else!"

"Everything like what?"

"Like Guatemalan antiquities!" she said, looking annoyed that she even had to say it.

"Maybe," he said.

"Well, what do you think?" She seemed almost angry now, as if she believed he was playing games with her.

"I'm not certain," said Joseph.

"Certainty isn't everything," said Kinsolving, always the mediator.

Gabriella took a sip of coffee and tried to control herself. "Then what's your opinion?" she asked him.

"I don't have an opinion. I just want to know how and why."

Kinsolving seemed to be quietly considering something. Then he piped up. "The problem with the New World people and the antagonisms surrounding Mundt's sausage plant have been a festering sore in my parish for a number of years. Maybe it's time it was brought to a head. Certain people in the community have been pressing for a town meeting to discuss the situation. Perhaps this is an appropriate time to set it up..."

"I'm surprised someone hasn't done that long ago," said Joseph.

"It's hard to break through the apathy," Kinsolving replied. He sounded as if this wasn't the first time he'd thought of it.

Gabriella shook her head. "We need to do something now. Meetings are fine, but we need to take action..."

"What do you suggest?" asked Kinsolving. Unlike Joseph, he looked truly interested.

"There's been a lot of smoke – mainly from them," she said. "Maybe it's time we started our own little fire."

"Here," said Joseph, taking his lighter out of his pocket, "I'll lend you my Ronson."

"I was thinking in metaphorical terms," she said, glowering at him. "The Power of the Press. But I wouldn't expect you to understand.."

"So," he said, as if he suddenly realized, "you want to write a novel!"

149

"I'm sorry," said Kinsolving, looking totally confused. "I'm afraid you lost me somewhere..."

"The Gazette," she said, turning to him and smiling, as if thankful that at least he leant a sympathetic ear. "We do have it at our disposal."

"Don't you think it would be a little dangerous going back there?" asked Kinsolving, raising his fatherly eyebrows.

"Maybe she hoped you had some muscle you could loan us," said Joseph, giving him a wink.

If he knew Joseph was kidding him, Kinsolving didn't let on. So perhaps he didn't. "I do have some friends who might help," he said.

Chapter 40

PANCHO ONE WAS about seven feet tall with a face like an accident. Pancho Two was shorter. About six foot ten. He had a jagged scar running across his forehead that looked like the zipper to the brain of Frankenstein. Pancho Three was skinny and maybe all of five foot four. He wore a T-shirt with sleeves pulled up so you could see his tattoo – a picture of a bloody knife with a message underneath which read, "FUCK WITH ME AND YOU'RE DEAD!"

"Nice friends you have," Joseph whispered to Kinsolving as the three braceros pulled up in front of the refuge driving a 1956 Ford pickup.

"Muscle you wanted. Muscle you got," said Kinsolving.

"What do you feed them? Raw meat on the bone?"

"Just watch what you say about Jose Cardinales," he said. "They're actually very sensitive."

They drove in convoy, the pickup following close behind Joseph's MG. Gabriella sat next to him with her lips tightly shut.

Even with the Three Panchos behind him, he still felt a rush of adrenaline when they reached the outskirts of Ecstasy. He kept waiting to hear the siren on Larson's Land Rover. Or worse the crack of a gun.

Maybe that's why Gabriella was so silent, he thought. Maybe her nerves were raw. Maybe the anticipation had her freaked.

But the town was quiet. Almost as if it was taking a late afternoon siesta. Strange, he thought. This was the North not the South. People up here didn't sleep. Not in the afternoon.

He looked behind him. The Three Panchos were sitting in the cab of the pickup having a ball. They were laughing and singing choruses of "La Cucaracha." They weren't frightened in the least. "What the hell!" Joseph thought to himself. "You only live once." And the way he was feeling, once was more than enough, anyhow.

They reached the Gazette without incident and parked. Gabriella lead the way to the office as the Three Panchos piled out of their pickup.

Down the road, some merchants looked out from their shops, peering at the procession like zombies from the village of the dead. One of the Panchos, the small one, turned in the direction of shadowland and shouted, "Hey! Ain't you never seen Mexicans before?"

Joseph thought to himself that they saw what they wanted to see. So probably they hadn't.

He half imagined the place would have been ransacked. But walking into the office, he saw that nothing seemed to have been touched. Everything appeared as they left it.

The three Panchos knew what was expected of them, having taken up positions outside the building. Joseph glanced around for a pack of smokes he had left lying around the other day. He found them, lit up and then tossed the pack out the open door to the scarfaced Pancho who grinned back at him like a bandito in some low budget film. When he closed the front door and turned around again, he noticed

Gabriella had disappeared.

He found her in the print shop.

She had opened the curtains. The late afternoon light was pouring through the glass and had lit up the center of the room giving the equipment a radiance that seemed to bring it to life.

The contrast was striking, he thought. Before, the place seemed like a museum. The press sat like a dusty relic of another era.

"Look at it," she said. "It's beautiful." She stood in quiet reverence as if witnessing something profound, a miracle like opening up a tomb and finding Gutenberg had risen from the dead.

There was definitely something about the light, Joseph thought. And even with his practised cynicism, he seemed to be taken by the seedy romance of it all.

He met her look and then wished he hadn't. It was one of those seductive jobs that he felt he could live without.

"Come on, Joseph," she said. "I know you love playing the hardboiled, coldhearted act. But you can't have lost all your spirit!"

A low blow. He still thought of himself as young at heart, except when he looked in the mirror.

She held out her youthful hand and motioned toward the printing press. "It's sitting there just waiting for us, Joseph. Can't you see? It's destiny..."

That was a word he truly hated. But he could see her point even though there was the horrible feeling he had just dropped into a Mills and Boon scenario without as much as a rubber for protection.

"Look," he said, "I don't mind stirring shit and the idea of rolling your own has a good down-home feel to it. But I don't like going off half-cocked. And frankly, I don't know where I am with all this yet..."

"But what do you want?" she asked in frustration. "I bet if you had this much dope in the safety of the City you'd be bragging to the other guys at Joe's, or wherever it is has-been hacks talk about the good old days, how you're going to win a Pulitzer!"

"Joe's closed down," he said. "And no one brags about winning a Pulitzer unless they're casting for a lead role in the remake of Front Page."

She stared at him hard and the look in her eyes was like a sneer – the kind that questions someone's manhood. "Sarcasm is like elevator shoes for puny minds. I think you're just afraid. Aren't you?"

Joseph dropped his cigarette, glanced down and ground it underfoot. "I'd be the last one to give a nickel if they wanted to build a statue of me holding out a sword and riding a stallion," he said, looking back up at her. "But this is your show, anyway, isn't it? So I'll make you a deal..."

"What?" she asked, the sneer quickly fading from her eyes.

"I don't like the ideas of mixing sausages and severed fingers. But sometimes you set things in motion and it works. Sometimes it flies back in your face and you have to eat crap..."

"What else is new?" she asked.

"Tell you what," he said. "I'll help you out under one condition..."

"Name it."

"That we let Kinsolving call his meeting. We tell them what we're going to do. If they agree, I'll help you run the press."

Chapter 41

KINSOLVING MADE SOME phone calls and was able to arrange for the use of the Grange Meeting Hall on Miller's Hill that evening. Even though it had fallen into disrepair after years of neglect, it was still structurally sound, he said.

Saez, the social worker from the migrant labor camp, was invited. Several people from the Salvador Garcia defence committee were asked to come, including Mildred Pike; and a few others, like Jane, the sad-eyed waitress, from town.

They all attended. Even Sheldon Beekman, who, at Kinsolving's insistence, made the long drive in from Mendicino.

Kinsolving acted as moderator and gave a summary of the series of events which led up to what he called "this festering abscess finally coming to a head."

Then he called upon Joseph to make some remarks.

Cringing at the idea of once more finding himself exactly where he didn't want to be, Joseph reluctantly stood up and muttered, "There's a lot of questions still unanswered, but it does seem clear that there's been a conspiracy going on which this town has ignored for the past ten years. Now the pot is on the boil, probably because of the Manning's investigation into the Salvador Garcia case and a few other events..." He stopped and stared at Gabriella.

"What isn't clear is how all these things are linked," he continued. "But at this point I'm not sure it matters..."

"Of course it matters!" Mildred Pike cut in. "I'm not interested in financial hanky-panky or politics. I want to get an innocent boy out of jail!"

"We all do, Mildred," said Kinsolving. "But at the moment this town seems to be in a state of undeclared war. It's a crisis situation and we have to deal with it..."

"There's a well of hostility that you're tapped, Radkin,"

said Saez. "I hope you're ready for the consequences..."

Joseph suddenly felt besieged. In fact, he agreed with Saez's remark. However, he found himself saying something else:

"What's happened has already happened. As I see it, you've really got only two choices left. You can do nothing and let them get away with murder. Or you can fight back."

Gabriella gave him a glowing smile.

"What are you suggesting, Radkin?" Beekman asked. "Pitched battles in the street?"

"Yeah, man, why not?" said one of the Panchos the one with the bloody tattoo. "Let's get it over with, man!"

"No, I don't want that," said Joseph, wondering, even as he spoke, what had gotten into him. "And they want it even less than we do. This town has been a gold mine for them, precisely because nobody ever made a fuss. Not a loud one, anyway. All I'm suggesting is to use the Gazette as it was meant to be used. Let's expose them for what they are..."

"Then what?" asked Saez.

"Then let's see what happens."

"Some plan," said Beekman.

"It sounds a little like a hit and run strategy, the way you proposed it," said Kinsolving. "I like the idea of using the paper as an organizing tool. But it has to lead to something. Perhaps we should call a larger meeting. Try to get everyone from the town..."

"We've tried to have meetings for years," said Mildred Pike. "Everybody has their own axe to grind and everybody gets mad at each other..."

"This time we got a live issue, though," said Seaz. "We could link it to the migrant labor situation..."

"Or that fuckin' sausage plant," said one of the Panchos.

Joseph looked over at Beekman and saw him shake his head and groan.

"Look," said Gabriella, finally speaking up. "First things first. Let's go with what we got. My own feeling is that they

155

can't stand the exposure..."

"Are you suggesting they're just going to pack their bags and go away?" asked Saez.

"No," she said. "But it's going to put a crimp in their style and might put pressure on the Feds to investigate!"

"She's right about that," said Kinsolving. "The government sometimes does need a little push. But the question is whether a story in a small town newspaper would be enough..."

"Joseph could get it picked up by the wire service," she said.

The assemblage turned toward him.

"Could you?" asked Kinsolving.

"Maybe," he said.

"Then you damn well better have your shit together," cautioned Beekman. "Because they probably have some high-priced lawyers on their team and they won't hesitate to hit you with everything they've got!"

Chapter 42

IT WAS AFTER the meeting dispersed that Joseph pulled Kinsolving and Beekman aside. When she saw them huddled in a corner, Gabriella come over to join them, too. "What would it take to get your friends in the Governor's office involved?" asked Joseph, looking at Kinsolving.

"I told you before," he said. "A smoking gun..."

"What do you think?" Joseph gritted his teeth and turned to Beekman.

"As far as I'm concerned," Beekman replied, "all you got are pots. But you don't have one to piss in."

"How about if we provide a smoking pot?" suggested

Gabriella.

"I'm not sure I know what you're talking about," said Kinsolving.

"I think I can get some documents that link the stuff being manufactured at the commune to the hot antiquities market..."

"From your insurance company?" asked Joseph.

"No," she said. "From someplace here in town. But it would take a little doing to get..."

"Maybe I shouldn't hear any more," said Beekman. "Then I can pretend to believe you when you call me from jail claiming to be innocent." He turned and started walking toward the door. "I'll meet you back at the refuge, Padre. I told Dash to call me there tonight."

"What have you got in mind?" asked Kinsolving, after Beekman walked out. He had a mischievous twinkle in his eye.

"Getting some cheese to bait a trap," Gabriella replied.

"Maybe you ought to take one of the Panchos," Kinsolving suggested.

She shook her head. "The fewer who know about this, the better." Then, looking at Joseph, she asked, "Will you come with me?"

"Of course he will!" said Kinsolving. Joseph gave him a dirty look. One which Gabriella didn't see or ignored. "Do you have a tool kit?" Gabriella asked Kinsolving. "Back at the refuge," he said. "Good," she replied. "There's a few things I want to get."

Chapter 43

GRIME'S CURIO SHOP was on River Drive. On one side of it was a secondhand clothing store. On the other was a place that sold fishing supplies. In front of the shop was a wooden Indian, dressed simply in a loincloth, holding out a rigid cigar. It was the kind they used to have in front of dime stores back in the good old days. But from its expression, the good old days hadn't really been that good, Joseph thought. Or maybe its wooden head ached from all the fat, balding fishermen making jokes about him through the years.

He parked the MG about fifty yards down the road. Getting out, he lifted up the hood and fixed it in an upright position.

"Why are you doing that?" Gabriella asked.

"You keep watch. If someone comes along and asks any questions, just say the car stalled out."

"I thought this was my show," she said.

"It is. But the cop around here has a sadistic gleam in his eye. And Beekman isn't going to be too quick getting you out of the slammer..."

She looked about as happy as the dime store Indian when he left her standing there and walked down to the river bank. There was a tow path that backed along the row of small buildings. He followed it till he came to the curio shop. Then he made his way up the grassy embankment to the rear of the store.

The back door of the shop was blocked by a giant garbage can. He pushed the can along the side of the building and then climbed on top to look inside a window. The window was curtained but as he balanced himself on the tottering can, he saw that the inside of the shop was dark.

As he tried to peer through the curtained window, he

suddenly heard the sound of footsteps. He turned to look, but his movement was too abrupt. The can slipped from under him, clattering down the concrete embankment like a steel drum loaded with firecrackers, and plunged into the water with a loud splash.

"Nice going," said a voice.

He looked over and saw her. "I thought you were going to keep watch by the car."

"I figured you might need some help," she said. "Why were you standing on the can?"

"I was looking to see what kind of burglar device they had..."

She looked down at the floating can. "I think the alarm already went off." Then turning back to him, she asked, "Did you want to get inside?"

"I thought that was the general idea..."

"Then you better do it fast," she said, leaning down, picking up a rock and then heaving it through the window.

He stared at her in amazement. "Are you crazy?" he shouted.

"I've been in here before," she said, knocking the jagged edges on the bottom of the window frame loose. "There's just a bunch of trinkets and junk. Nothing of value. Certainly not enough to warrant a burglar alarm." She finished cleaning the particles of glass from the ledge. Then, turning to him she said, "Give me a boost up."

He didn't move. He just kept staring at her, as if trying to figure something out.

"Come on!" she said. "We've got to work fast!"

He came over and cupped his hands. "Deja vu," he said to himself.

She moved smoothly, first undoing the catch and sliding the window open and then easing herself up and over the casement, swinging her body so when she dropped on the floor inside, she landed on her feet.

Then she disappeared into the darkness.

159

A few seconds later, the back door opened. She motioned to him. "Hurry up!"

As he stepped over the threshold, she opened the bag which was slung over her shoulder and pulled out a flashlight.

Switching on the light, she kept the beam low, toward the ground.

"Follow me," she said. "His office is the first door on the left."

She found it quickly enough, but the door was locked.

Taking a chisel and hammer from her bag, she handed them to him and then focused the flashlight on the keyhole. "It's a flimsy catch. Just smash it open!"

"Convenient," he said. "You always carry these things around?"

"That's what I went with Kinsolving to get," she said. "Do you want me to do it?"

"Be my guest," he replied. "You seem to be the expert."

Taking the tools back, she placed the thin blade of the chisel by the mortise, while he held the flashlight, and gave the end a smack with the hammer. The door swung open.

"His files are in the far corner of the room, next to the desk," she said.

He moved the beam of light along the wall till he found the metal files. She moved quickly, striding over and then pulling open each drawer until she found the one that was locked.

Prying the drawer open, she pulled the files out, stacking them on the floor. Joseph watched her rifle through them until she found a certain folder.

"This is what we want."

She stuffed the file into her bag and then looked over to where he was holding the light, watching her in quiet wonder.

"Let's get the hell out of here!" she said.

Chapter 44

RUMMAGING THROUGH THE boxes of type, Joseph tried to remember some of the tricks he had learned those many years ago when he was learning to grow a moustache and writing grand opuses by candle light. He and his buddies were so fascinated with the magic of the printed word that they had bought an old press and a box of rusty type for twenty bucks. They ran off a hundred copies of a magazine called "Bayside Blues" which they hawked on the streets for two bits a shot. Then it folded and that was that.

Except the smell of printer's ink stayed with him. And even later, when he became a real journalist – the kind who would have bought a copy of Bayside Blues and then tossed it in the nearest trash can – he loved to go down to the press room just to take a whiff. It was like the most seductive perfume imaginable, he thought.

Meanwhile, Gabriella was furiously typing away, churning out copy. She wrote about Mundt's sausage house scam and the Indian village that was used to provide the fakes which were then sold to dealers for extraordinary prices.

"The evidence," she wrote, "is in a document that has come into our possession. It gives the catalogue code of various artefacts, the prices and the dealers who provide these fakes to wealthy collectors and museums. The catalogue numbers all refer to forgeries that were distributed through Mundt and Grimes and produced by the New World Commune. The Gazette has forwarded this document to the proper authorities so that they may continue the investigation into this scandal which is certain to shake antiquities markets throughout the world..."

"Not bad," said Joseph, doing a quick editing job as he read over her draft. "But it's short. What else have you got?"

"How about a story on Salvador Garcia?" she said.

They did it straight away, telephoning Mildred Pike, Kinsolving and even Beekman and interviewing them about the case.

"A Sad Miscarriage of Justice," was the headline Joseph set. And, as a subheading, he set some slightly smaller type which read, "Young Man Rots In Jail While Jurors Plead For His Release. Friends Confident Of Victory On Appeal."

He showed it to her. "Objective?" he asked.

"No," she replied. "But did we want it to be?"

He shook his head. "Anything else? You still have lots of space to fill."

She thought a minute. Then she said, "Maybe I'll do something on Mayan fruits the commune is growing. That's another link with Mundt. Remember those magnificent strawberries I found warehoused at his sausage plant? I bet they came from there!"

It took the rest of the night to finish setting type, with Joseph blocking it through trial and error, proofing and re-blocking again until at last he got it right.

Then they let it roll. It was beauty in motion, he thought.

They had enough paper for five hundred copies of a broadsheet. After spoilage, it left them with three hundred and some. They had started around midnight. By five in the morning, exhausted, their hands and face coated thickly with black ink, they finally were done.

She put her arm around him as she held up a finished copy. "An historic occasion, don't you think?"

He read aloud the editorial she had written. "This is the final issue of a great newspaper, dedicated to the memory of Elizabeth and Felix Manning and all those who came before them. The Gazette is now bequeathed to the people of Ecstasy, with the hope that one of you will find the inspiration to pick up the gauntlet and continue..."

"Well," he said, "you did it." He smiled.

"That's the first time I ever saw you smile," she said.

162

"Really?" He was honestly surprised. "Maybe I figured you deserved it."

"Thanks," she said.

"You got stacks of them," he pointed to the bundles. "Have you thought about how you're going to get it delivered?"

"Oh, that's all arranged. The Three Panchos volunteered. They hate Mundt and the New World people as much as we do..."

"Good luck," he said, with an extended yawn.

"Joseph," she said, "There's something I want to tell you..." She was gazing into his eyes and he thought he saw something he didn't want to see.

"Save it for the morning. Both of us need some sleep," he said.

Chapter 45

THERE IS "REAL time", the time we use when we set our watch. There is "fantasy time" which is time manipulated to make us believe the otherwise unbelievable. And there is "dream time" which inhabits another world out of our control – one that can't be ordered. So dream time is a paradox.

Joseph was deep into this paradox where real time and fantasy time were battling it out, when suddenly he heard someone knock. At first, it was hard to decide which world he should let the knocker enter. Fortunately, the decision was made for him.

The biggest Pancho burst into the storeroom. "Excuse me, senior. It's the Padre..."

"He's here?" said Joseph, glancing at his watch and surprised to see the hour.

"No, senior, he's on the phone. He say it's mucho importante."

Dragging himself out of bed, Joseph made his way to the office and picked up the receiver.

Kinsolving's voice sounded hoarse, as if he, too, had been up all night. "Some very curious things are happening," he said. "I think we need to talk..."

"I'm listening," said Joseph.

"You better come over here," Kinsolving said. "I don't want to say anything over the phone."

He threw some water on his face and changed his underclothes.

Before he left, he scribbled out a note to Gabriella.

Chapter 46

KINSOLVING WAS ON the phone to someone else when Joseph arrived at the refuge. He went into the refectory to wait. There was a steaming pot of coffee. He poured himself a cup and breathed in the caffeinated aroma before tasting a drop.

When Kinsolving came in to meet him, Joseph could tell he was extremely upset. In fact, the contrast to his usual easygoing demeanour was striking. It looked to Joseph as if Kinsolving had a message from God last night saying that He didn't exist.

"What's up?" asked Joseph, offering the priest a cigarette.

Kinsolving accepted the fag and a light and then shook his head, while taking a puff.

"Some very strange things have been happening..." he began.

"Like what?"

"Firstly, I got a call from Saez late last night. He said someone's been spreading rumors that more bodies have been found in the fields, butchered in a way that suggest ritual sacrifice. There's also been some leaflets circulated, saying the migrant laborers are responsible for the disappearance of several teenagers..."

"According to Saez, that's happened before."

"Not in such an organized way. It's very worrying..."

"What else happened?" Joseph prompted.

"I also got a call from Steven Roper..."

"Who's he?"

"A friend of Miles Tippett the translator we spoke about..."

"Yes, I had a very strange meeting with him the other day," said Joseph.

"You did?" Kinsolving raised his eyebrows in a look of extreme surprise. "When was that?"

"The day before yesterday. Tippett phoned the newspaper. Gabriella set up an interview with a lot of conditions..."

"Then you actually met him?" said Kinsolving. "That's very curious..."

"'Met' is probably too strong a word. Anyway, you were telling me about the call you got from Roper..."

"Roper is another disenchanted missionary who worked with the Marsden Institute. He left the same time as Tippett. In fact, they shared a room here at the refuge for a while before they found a place..."

"You helped them both hide out?"

"Yes."

"Are they still living together?"

"Theoretically. But when Roper phoned he said he was very worried about Tippett. He said Tippett had been gone for several days and he was concerned about what happened to him. It's dreadfully important, you see, because we were depending on his testimony for the appeal in the Salvador Garcia case. However, now that you tell me you saw him..."

"Actually, I didn't see anyone. He kept himself hidden..." Joseph rubbed the bristles on his chin. "Does Tippett drive a black sedan?"

"Tippett doesn't drive," said Kinsolving. "Neither does

Roper. I know that because I had to chauffeur them around for a while, till they got settled. Why do you ask?"

"Because whoever I spoke with jumped into a black sedan afterwards and drove off."

"Then you didn't speak with Tippett," said Kinsolving. He looked even more uneasy now. "That's another curiosity to add to the list..."

"What else?"

"I saw Salvador yesterday. He was terribly worried. Extremely agitated, in fact..."

"About what?"

"He told me that the 11Ahau katun is coming up..."

"You've lost me again, Padre," Joseph said.

"The Mayan cycle of time. It has to do with the past repeating itself in periods of harvest and joy and periods of famine and plague. The 11Ahau katun is supposed to be very bad..."

Kinsolving stopped for a moment. Then he said, "Do you remember that congregation of Indians camping out in front of the prison?"

"Yes," said Joseph, recalling the image of the stoic-faced people silently waiting, as if bearing witness to something no one could see but them.

"Beekman told me the group has doubled in size over the last day. And the mood has changed dramatically. There's a sense of anticipation now, as if they expect something to happen very soon."

"But those other Indians standing watch – they aren't Mayan, are they?"

"No, they're not. They seem to be from many tribes..."

"So what's it about?" asked Joseph.

Kinsolving looked out into the distance, as if his mind was drifting to another universe. "Sometimes things happen that are beyond our control," he said. "They happen and we're swept up by the events like being caught in a cyclone. People who are exceptionally in tune with nature often sense these things before they take place..."

"That's a little too metaphysical for me," said Joseph, lighting up a cigarette. "I live in a more bread and butter world..."

"We define the world in the way it makes sense to us," Kinsolving replied. "I don't know what's going on either, but I'm very concerned..."

"But you didn't call me up this morning to tell me about vague fears, did you?" asked Joseph.

"You're right," said Kinsolving, looking at him as if to ask for his understanding. "I wanted to plead with you to wait on the newspaper. I thought it over again last night. This area is like a tinder box. I don't want us to be responsible for providing the spark that sets it off..."

"I know what you mean," said Joseph, flicking his cigarette and gazing at the glowing ember, "and I thought of that myself. But we've been swept up in a cyclone ourselves..."

"And the newspaper?" he asked.

"Unfortunately, they've all been sent out."

Chapter 47

HIS MIND WAS going through gymnastics as he drove back to the Gazette. Kinsolving's anxiety had been contagious. On the other hand, he prided himself on a certain commitment to rational thought. Not that he didn't believe in intuition. That was a journalist's prime asset. But being an investigative journalist meant that cause and effect relationships needed to be more substantive than what was foretold by the stars. Unless you were writing the astrology column.

One thing that came up in his conversation was preying on him – the mystery concerning the translator, Miles Tippett. It had been bothering him ever since he had gone with Gabriella on that curious interview. His suspicions were aroused, making him determined to finally do something he had been wanting to for a while. It involved a piece of research. And it demanded he go back to San Francisco.

By the time he arrived at the Gazette, he had convinced himself that he needed to make the long drive south. But a queasy feeling in his stomach told him that he shouldn't be gone too long.

He went into the office to tell Gabriella.

The office was empty. Not even the Three Panchos were around.

He went back to the print shop and knocked at the door which led to her room.

"Gabriella?" he called out.

There wasn't any reply.

He opened the door and looked in. It was empty.

Walking inside, he looked around. All her things were gone.

He opened the closet. The clothes racks were bare.

On the floor of the closet, however, sat an old portable typewriter. He picked up the typewriter and put it on the wooden table Gabriella had used as a desk. Then, rolling in a piece of paper, he proceeded to type out a note.

When he was done, he took the paper out and inspected it carefully. Afterwards, he folded it in half, stuck it in his pocket, closed the case and placed the typewriter back in the closet.

He was about to leave when he noticed an envelope on the floor by the edge of the bed. He went over and picked it up. The envelope was empty, but on the back someone had pencilled a name – Vivian Galinski – and a telephone number with a dialing code for San Francisco.

He made a note of the name and the phone number. But he didn't really need to. For Vivian Galinski was someone he knew well.

Chapter 48

IT WAS MID-AFTERNOON by the time he reached San Francisco. The frantic race to the bridges by anxious commuters crazed by various hormonal imbalances hadn't begun yet. Even so, the congestion was such that Joseph was struck by the contrast. Ecstasy, he thought, might be hell but at least there was a parking space.

He had known Vivian Galinski from the old days at the daily. She was one of those bright-eyed, unstoppable women with a mission. Unfortunately, she kept changing her mind as to what that mission was. One day she was a journalist and a damn good one, he thought. Then she disappeared. The next time he saw her, she was a member of the bar.

Columbus Towers was a curiously anachronistic building where Galinski now held court amongst the artdeco. It straddled two worlds. One side faced the postmodern monstrosities of the financial district which leered over the rest of the city like a gang of star warriors about to rape the universe. The other side cozied up to North Beach and what remained of urban bohemia. So the building, he thought, summed up nicely the city's schizophrenia.

Galinski's office was the size of a cracker box. With her cluttered desk, stacks of cardboard files and her forest of potted plants, there was hardly space for a client to fit in.

She met him at the door and gave him a hug and a kiss. "Radkin, you old sweetiepie!" she gushed. "Where the hell have you been the last fifteen years?"

"Give me a second to look through my diary," he responded. And then, glancing at the cluttered mess, he said, "Nice place you got."

"At least I didn't end up there," she said, pointing out the window to the concrete launching pad of the TransAmerica rocket.

She motioned to a chair cowering next to a luscious rhododendron. "Take the weight off your feet if you don't mind sitting next to Harriet."

He sat down in the chair, pushing back the shrub so he could see. Galinski perched herself on the edge of her desk and looked down at him. "I thought of you when I heard about the Mannings," she said. "I seemed to recall that you and Elizabeth were good friends..."

"We went around together for a while when I was going to university. Lost touch and met up again at the newspaper. By that time she was with Felix. You were their lawyer?" he asked.

"On and off," she said. "I helped Felix with his suit against the daily. We managed to get some compensation but not much..." She stood up and walked behind her desk, sitting down on her swivel chair. "That was a pretty lousy deal. You remember?"

"Sure," he said. "How could I forget?"

"Of course. You were one of the only people there who stood up for him, weren't you?"

"He stepped on a few toes and one of the toes just happened to be connected to an important foot. It was a nothing story about some stupid purchases the art museum made. The head of the museum was the publisher's brother. He got a little incensed and ordered Felix to back off. Felix told him to get lost and he was fired. I didn't give a shit about the story or about Felix. But it was a matter of principle..."

"You should have come to see me," she said. "I could have sued the goullies off them..."

Joseph shrugged. "By that time I was ready to leave anyway..."

"It doesn't matter. All these people care about is money. They're not bothered about principles unless you follow it up with a cash demand."

"Whatever," said Joseph, pulling out his pack of cigarettes.

"It's something better off forgotten." He pushed at the leaf which kept falling in his face. "Does Harriet mind if I smoke?"

"She probably does," said Galinski. "If you have such an urgent death wish, why don't you stand over by the window."

He did as she asked and lit up a cigarette while looking out at the monuments to turn-of-the-millennium power. "What kind of work did you do for Felix?" he asked.

"After the suit? Not much. I'd run into him now and then at the Roma or the Puccini. There was a time he was asking my advice about some investments..."

Joseph made a face. "The guy had money to burn, didn't he?"

"Not really," she said. "It seemed to me he was always up and down. Sometimes he had money and sometimes he was broke."

"I thought he came from a wealthy family," said Joseph, turning to look at her and showing his surprise.

"He did. In fact, when they died they left him a bundle. But he managed to go through it pretty fast. At least, that's what he told me."

Flicking the ash from his cigarette out the window, he stopped to watch it float through the air, down to the street below. "That advice on investments what was it about?" he asked.

"Art, of course. It was the only thing he knew anything about. That and archaeology. He was fascinated by the extraordinary rise in prices in the antiquities markets. He had this idea of starting some sort of consortium having to do with antiquities futures..."

"Antiquities futures?" asked Joseph, looking at her as if he didn't understand.

"You know, like the commodities market. You place bets on whether the price will go up or down. You can do it with anything oil, pork bellies ... so Felix wondered why you couldn't do it with antiquities."

"Could you?" he asked.

"Of course. But I couldn't help him set it up. I'm not really into that kind of financial hanky-panky."

"And that's the last you saw of him?"

"For a while," she said. "Then I saw him again. Just a few months ago. He asked me to do a few things for him..."

"Like what?"

She was silent, as if she were thinking some things over. "I don't know, Joseph it's pretty strange..."

"Listen," he said, "I'm not asking you to betray any confidences. But I'd appreciate anything you can tell me as a friend."

"It's not that, Joseph. I know I can trust you," she said, picking up a pencil and fingering it, nervously.

"Yeah," he muttered. "I'm loyal as a dog..."

She scribbled a few doodles on a piece of paper and then took a deep breath and said, "It was about a month ago. He came to see me about redoing his will..."

"Just out of the blue?" Joseph asked.

"Yes. He said he'd been thinking about it for a long time and he decided he shouldn't procrastinate any longer..."

"But why then?"

"I don't know," she said, looking down at the desk. "Maybe he was ill. Maybe he had a premonition."

"Had you done a will for him before?"

She shook her head. "The curious thing about it was the second beneficiary he chose."

"The first was Elizabeth, I suppose. Who was the second?"

"Some archaeological institute based in Belize."

He was beginning to feel an ache in his head. He was dying for a drink. "Who's the executor, Vivian?" he asked.

"Professor Stanton. He was a colleague of Felix's at the university."

"Which university was Felix at? I've forgotten."

"The University of California at Davis. But Stanton moved down to LA. In fact, Stanton is one of the directors at the Belize institute. My understanding is that he's down there now."

"Who are you dealing with then about the will, I mean..."

"His secretary."

"At the university?"

"I suppose. I just leave messages for him on his answering machine. She gets back to me."

"What's her name?"

"I don't know. She just refers to herself as 'Mr. Stanton's secretary.' I haven't really had much dealings with her..."

The ache in his head was getting worse. He lit up another cigarette. "Vivian," he asked, "has the coroner made his report yet on the identity of the bodies?"

"I'm expecting it any day now," she replied. "They were waiting for the dental reports for positive identification. But they weren't forthcoming..."

"Why?"

"The dentist claims he couldn't find them."

"That seems a little odd, don't you think?" said Joseph, giving her a serious look.

"I agree," she said, pursing her lips and staring back at him.

"So what happens about the coroner's report, I mean..."

"The coroner will make a judgement based on the circumstantial evidence. Two bodies found, one male, one female, the approximate age and height of the residents. Without any evidence to the contrary, I'm sure he'll decide that Felix and Elizabeth were the people who died in the fire..." She stopped and looked into his eyes. "Do you have any evidence to the contrary, Joseph?"

He shook his head. "What about their relatives? What do they have to say?"

"Felix's parents are dead. Elizabeth's mother lives in Oakland. She's been informed. But I advised her not to see the body. It's a pretty gruesome sight. Of course, she was very distraught."

"It must have been hard on her." Joseph glanced out of the window again. "Hannah's a fine woman..."

"You know her?" asked Galinski.

"I knew her many years ago," said Joseph. "I should look her up…"

Chapter 49

HIS HOUSE WAS still empty when he got back and went inside. He fixed himself a drink and checked his answering machine for messages and then lay down on the couch. He lay there for an hour, looking up at the ceiling, inspecting the cracks. Certain things began clicking in his mind. But for every mental door he opened, there seemed to be two others that stayed shut.

After a while, he got up again and, pouring himself another drink, picked up the phone. First he checked in with the wire service, just to let Tarzan know he was still alive. Then he phoned the archaeology department at Davis and set up an appointment to see someone. Lastly, he phoned Elizabeth's mother.

"Of course I remember," she said. "It's very kind of you to call."

"If you don't mind having visitors," he told her, "I'd like to drop by…"

Chapter 50

IT WAS A small cottage set in the Oakland hills near the border of Berkeley and it had one of those magnificent panoramic views that certain Californians would die for.

Parking his car in the drive, Joseph recalled the days

many years before when he would peddle his bicycle up here without so much as a second thought. Now it was tiring for him drive.

Below the crystal waters of the bay spread out in patches – a thousand lakes meeting the sky in a crescendo of fantasy blue. Further on, the horizon was dominated by the geometric outline of San Francisco, like the basic shapes in a set of children's building blocks. And in his mind he compared it to the view from Miller's Hill in Ecstasy.

As he walked to the door, Joseph could hear the haunting strains of a piano concerto by Erik Satie. It triggered the memory of some very comfortable evenings, sitting by the fire, drinking brandy and reading Baudelaire aloud while wondering what it would be like to walk a lobster through the streets of Paris. And through the mist of time, he could hear the echo of laughter.

He pushed the button for the bell and heard the chimes mix discordantly with Satie. The door opened and there was the face he remembered so well, etched in his memory for over twenty years – the tiny, sparrowlike woman with twinkling eyes.

Taking her wrinkled hand, he gave it a squeeze. "Hello, Hannah," he said.

"It's so wonderful to see you, Joseph. After all these years!" she said, as she ushered him in.

It still looked the same, he thought, glancing around. The paintings of Rousseau and Chagall – the dreamers, the weavers of mythical innocence, she used to say. The piano polished so bright you could almost see the music reflected in the wood. The bookshelves, with row upon row of books – leatherbound, paperback, new and tattered which reached right up to the ceiling. And the stacks of newspapers and journals that rested by the side.

"Nothing has changed," he said, running his finger along a row of books until he found one that he knew.

"'Nothing has changed and everything has changed.'

175

Isn't that what we used to say, Joseph? It was our response to that tired aphorism of the French, 'The more things change, the more they stay the same.'"

He looked at her and wondered how someone who had lost so much hiding out in France during the war only to be turned over to the Gestapo, the concentration camps, the death of her husband, coming to America with a tiny daughter – how someone like that could continue to go on with such dignity was a mystery to him.

"I was going through her things and found this," said Hannah, sitting down on the couch and taking a scrapbook from the coffee table. Joseph sat down next to her as she opened it up.

"She was such a wonderful artist," said Hannah, turning the pages slowly and passing through the years; paging through her daughter's life.

He watched in fascination as the pictures went from childlike scribbles, the joyous outpouring of youth, through the mannered art school poses, to the search for identity of teenagehood.

She stopped at a self-portrait Elizabeth had done when she was sixteen years old, by the date at the bottom. It was a very different Elizabeth than he had known just four years later. It was the eyes and mouth that fascinated him. They were filled with the torment of growing up.

"What was she like back then?" asked Joseph.

Hannah pointed to a poem which was scribbled underneath the drawing. "I think that says it all, don't you?"

The poem read:

"My lips have tasted bitter fruit
My heart is filled with lies
The venom of a soft embrace
Has clouded up my eyes."

It was a poem he would have rejected when he was editing the Bayside Blues, but, with the picture, it did sum up those dreadful adolescent years, as Hanah suggested.

"One thing I always wanted to ask you," he said, turning to look at the elderly woman. "Why did you name her Elizabeth?"

"I didn't," she replied. "It was a name she chose herself when she turned thirteen and decided she wanted to be English..."

"And she stuck with it," said Joseph.

"She was very stubborn," Hannah confirmed, with a note of pride.

Joseph stared into her eyes and wondered where she was she had such a faraway look.

"Hannah," he said, "you know there was never any positive identification of the body. Do you think it's possible she's still alive?"

Hannah shook her head. "I thought of that, myself, Joseph. But if she were alive, I'd know it. Somehow, she'd have let me know, wouldn't she?"

Chapter 51

THE DAVIS BRANCH of the University of California was about sixty miles north along the highway that led to Redding. It had started academic life as an agricultural college serving the farming enterprises of the Sacramento valley. But corn and cows were soon supplemented by medicine and then a growing range of pursuits. By the 70's, it had become another competitor for the jewels offered to university crowns thanks to a Swedish dynamite merchant.

Professor Sinclair, who was head of the archaeology department, wasn't a Nobel winner. But he came close, having been lured from Cambridge with offers of a king's ransom in any currency of his choice. Somehow, though, even with an unwanted swimming pool and a house that was twenty times as big as his dinky flat in England, he had managed to keep is priorities straight as a Yeoman's ramrod.

"I've begun to question quite seriously the idea of California," he told Joseph, as they strolled down the hall toward his office. "I despise what's happening to the soil of its earth, the water of its rivers and the brains of its people."

"Did you ever think of going back to England?" Joseph asked.

"Yes," Sinclair replied. "Every day. The problem is that I hate what's happening there even more."

"So what's your alternative?" Joseph wanted to know as much for himself as anything.

"Fortunately, I have a rather cozy retreat in the past. Otherwise I'd go insane..."

Looking at the man's ruddy face and jolly eyes, Joseph seriously doubted he'd really go bonkers. But he knew what Sinclair meant. "Would you have rather been a Mayan?" he asked.

Sinclair stopped suddenly and looked at him as if he had considered the possibility. "The problem is the difference between looking at something outside in, rather than inside out. 'To be' and 'to understand' seem to be mutually exclusive." Then, turning sprightly on his toes, he opened a door.

The office he ushered Joseph into was a large airy space – privileges of rank, Joseph supposed – filled with rocks and bones and masks, but somehow managing to avoid that cloistered feel of decaying artefacts.

"Make yourself comfortable." Sinclair pointed to an empty chair. Then, looking slightly confused, he said, "What did you want to see me about again?"

"A colleague of yours – he once was, anyway. Felix Manning..."

"Ah, yes, Manning..." Sinclair's eyes lit up as he shook his mane of greying hair. "Quite a chap."

"You knew him well, I guess."

"Well enough."

"Does that mean you liked him or didn't?"

Sinclair's laugh was infectious. His whole body seemed to participate in the amusement. "The word 'like' is a curious one, don't you think? It comes from the old Anglo-Saxon 'lician' or 'gelician' which means 'to please.' So, did he please me?" Sinclair mulled it over and then answered, "On occasion."

In Joseph's way of speaking, that meant nothing at all. So he pursued the real question. "Was he good at his job?"

"That depends on what his job was." Sinclair scratched his head and gave off a puzzled look. "And, actually, that was never very clear to me..."

"But aren't you head of the department?" asked Joseph.

"A big mistake. Never should have done it. But it's so unpleasant, we decided to toss it around, two years at a crack rather like a prison stretch. Thank God my time is almost done!"

He'd met elusive politicians before, but Sinclair, he thought, put them all to shame. This man had truly mastered the art of never giving a straight reply.

But just as Joseph thought he had him figured, Sinclair turned right around and said, "So what is it you really want?"

"To know a little more about the Mayans, I guess," he said, somewhat taken aback. "And about Manning's involvement with them."

"His involvement was recent. But people often come to things late in their lives. I understand he began his career a an art historian."

"Is that usual for the two disciplines to mix?"

"Quite. Especially in archaeometry, which was Manning's specialization..."

Joseph shook his head. "Archaeometry? What's that?"

"It's the science of verification – the study of techniques which allow us to ascertain whether something is ten years old or ten thousand. But precise dating is just part of it. There's the study of materials, of earthen sediments, of metallurgy

179

anything that would give the archaeologist an indication of whether what he dug up is an important find or not."

"So an archaeometrist is who you would go to in order to see if something you were given is a fake?"

"If you wanted to have it tested, yes. They have a number of laboratory techniques at their disposal. Not fail-safe, of course. There's always enormous room for error..."

"Was Felix considered an authority?"

"He had a growing reputation. Especially after the codex find..."

"Yes, the Mayan codex," said Joseph. "I heard of that. But I thought there were only four in existence..."

"In the last year the number reached five. Caused quite a stir in our little pre-Columbian world. The question, though, was one of verification. There were two, you see, which had roughly the same provenance..."

"A cave in Guatemala?"

"Yes," said Sinclair. "So you know about it?"

"Not much. Are you saying that Felix verified the codex?"

"One of them. Of course, it was a great sensation."

"How much would you say the codex was worth?"

"It was priceless. As long as there wasn't a question of forgery."

"But I thought you said that Felix verified it."

"He did. But when word surfaced of the other codex with the same provenance, it cast a seed of doubt. One of them was bound to be a forgery..."

"These two codexes – who has them?"

"One is controlled by a consortium. The other by a missionary group."

"The New World Church."

"Yes."

"Has the one from the New World Church been tested and verified?"

"To my knowledge, it hasn't been presented for verification yet. Except that a small fragment was sent for carbon dating. That fragment was verified to be over a thousand years old..."

"The paper, you mean..."

"The paper, yes."

"But I understand that a cache of ancient paper was found in the cave that was excavated. Couldn't it have been used to forge the New World codex?"

"It's possible to have forged both," said Sinclair.

Joseph thought for a moment. Then he asked. "Are both these codexes exactly the same?"

"No," said Sinclair. "They differ in one crucial respect – the date of reckoning."

"I'm not sure what that means," Joseph said.

Sinclair pointed to a chart posted on the wall, with what looked to be meshed gears composed of hieroglyphic symbols and signs. "Here's a schematic diagram of the Mayan notion of time, the interlocking calendars of the Sun, Venus and the sacred calendar which combined 13 diefied numbers with 20 named days. The Venus almanac was a combination of 65 Venus cycles joined with 146 sacred cycles. It was used to determine a propitious time for ritual combat and sacrifice."

Joseph tried to make sense of the gibberish and decided he'd probably have to pour over it an hour before he could understand. "So what's the date of reckoning you were talking about?" he asked.

"The Mayans had a strong sense of cycles, of the past continually repeating itself and, in a sense, becoming the future. For them, seeing into the future, was to study the past. The past and the future merged into one. For example, the Spanish rule melded into a previous conquest by the Itza. And Christianity merged into the worship of the Kukulca, another alien religion forced on the Maya 600 years earlier. For them, time receded into a past so remote that we can barely comprehend it, but always in cycles which could be predicted by their almanacs."

"Then the future was always foretold," said Joseph. "What happened to their ideology when it wasn't?"

"They believed that history repeats itself only when certain influences are in balance. For example, they thought that the world would come to a sudden end when an overpowering combination of evil influences marked the termination of a time period. The period of time that was of most importance to the Maya was a katun – twenty years. But, because of the intermeshing of the thirteen sacred days, a katun could only end on the day "Ahau" coupled with a certain sacred number. Therefore a katun of a given name was repeated every 260 tuns or 257 of our years. The day of reckoning was when the evil influences were at their height. And they believed that day to be on the 11 Ahau katun."

"What happened then?" Joseph asked.

"The worst that could happen is that the world would come to an end."

"You mean Armageddon."

"Except the Mayans believed that the world ended and was recreated five times already. We're into our sixth go-around."

"So how do they know which 11 Ahau is the last?"

"It was in the hands of the gods. If they weren't appeased, then the world would end."

"You mean sacrificing to them," said Joseph. "Would they accept goats or did they need humans?"

"The more evil abounded, the greater was the sacrifice that was needed. Humans, yes. But never on the same scale as the Aztec."

"Who was chosen?" Joseph asked. "I suppose not too many volunteered."

"You'd be wrong," Sinclair replied. "The greatest honor was to sacrifice yourself for the sake of your people. This, after all, was a society of true believers. If you believed you could save the world by sacrificing yourself, I mean truly believed, wouldn't you do it?"

Joseph thought for a moment and then he said, "It's hard to think of being a true believer anymore."

"Perhaps that's our problem," he said, "but I should remind you that the blood sacrifice is alive and well. All we've done is transfer the rhetoric from the needs of the gods to the needs of the state."

"OK," said Joseph, "but if the day of reckoning according to the Mayan calendar is 11 Ahau, then what about the New World codex?"

"The day of reckoning in that one, I understand, coincides more with the Christian millennium." Sinclair gave a significant rise of his eyebrows.

"Then clearly the New World codex is a fraud," Joseph said.

"I would have thought that most people would have accepted that to be the case. However, the New World people have managed to gather a distinguished group of supporters."

"Legitimate scientists?"

Sinclair chuckled. "What is a legitimate scientist? Someone who's able to get large government grants? Someone who's given a chair at a prestigious university?"

Joseph stood up. "Well, thanks for the lecture, doc," he said. "Before I go, I wonder if you could do me one more favor..."

"Anyone who could sit through my lecture with such rapt interest deserves a favor," he replied. "What can I do for you?"

"I'd like to see where Manning had his office."

"That's easily done," said Sinclair, walking over to the door and opening it up. "It's right down the hall. Just next to the anatomy lab."

"Human anatomy?" asked Joseph, looking at him.

"Yes, we share the space with the medical facilities. Archaeologists do have to know quite a bit about the subject."

"I suppose," said Joseph, as Sinclair escorted him down

183

the hallway. And more to himself than the professor, he muttered, "Strange that his office butted up against it."

"We've had lots of mysteries around here lately. Just last week, two cadavers disappeared from the anatomy lab..." Sinclair seemed to delight in this gossip, as if this information was far more exciting than a bag of bones.

"Two?" said Joseph. "Is there a good resale value in dead bodies these days?"

"Not ones soaked in formaldehyde," said Sinclair. "Then another mystery right around that time we lost half our staff..."

"Who else besides Manning?"

"Professor Stanton. He went down to that institute in Belize..."

"What is it, exactly?"

"I don't know much about it, but I understand a group of academics made representation to the government of Belize. They asked for permission to engage in a massive project into the resurrection of a lost Mayan city."

"Financed by whom?" asked Joseph.

"I don't know," Sinclair replied. "But they seem to be well funded."

"How long would a project like that take?"

"Unearthing the remains of a magnificent Mayan city? It would be a lifetime's work," he said. "And also the opportunity of one's life if you're a dedicated archaeologist."

"So there was Manning and Stanton who left all of a sudden. Was there someone else?"

"Yes. We lost our graduate assistant. A lovely young woman..."

"What was her name?" asked Joseph.

"What was her name?" Sinclair repeated, tapping a finger on his nose. Suddenly the bulb in his head lit up. "Oh, yes. Genevieve Lumly," he said. "That was her name. Genevieve Lumly. Lovely name. Delightful girl..."

"I'm sure she was," Joseph muttered. Then, shaking

hands with Stanton, he said, "Thanks for all your trouble, doc."

"Not at all," said Stanton, walking him to the outside door. "We don't have many visitors with such a curious fascination about ancient civilizations any more and it's very peculiar you came on this particular day. Very peculiar indeed..."

"My fascination is pretty new," Joseph admitted, opening the door and then looking back. "But why is it so peculiar?"

"Didn't I tell you?" Sinclair asked, looking like someone who forgot to put on his trousers.

"Tell me what?"

"The Mayan date, 11Ahau. It's right about now."

"You mean today?" he asked, looking at Sinclair questioningly.

"Today, tomorrow, sometime soon. Our calendars don't perfectly match. It's hard to be precise when you translate theirs into ours."

"But you don't believe in that mumbo-jumbo, do you?" asked Joseph.

"Why are their ideas any more mumbo-jumbo than ours?" he asked. "They had a much longer history in which to test their theories. And the basis of their cosmology is very painstaking research into the movement of the planets and the stars. Our science is just beginning to understand how this tiny planet earth is influenced by other forces in the universe that there are cycles beyond the control of man and beast – rhythms of nature like tidal forces, which affect our lives. Most midwives know that births increase twofold during the period of a full moon. Doctors still have trouble accepting that idea..."

Sinclair pointed out to the grazing lands which adjoined the campus. "The Chinese have decided that animals are better predictors of major seismic events than humans. They have teams of observers whose job it is to watch for strange reactions in the grazing patterns of sheep and cattle. Yesterday, I saw a cow trying to climb a tree out there. Have you

185

ever witnessed a cow trying to climb a tree, Mr. Radkin?"

Joseph shook his head. "Don't think I have," he answered.

"It's quite a sight," said Sinclair, his eyes twinkling brightly. "Quite a sight, indeed..."

Chapter 52

IT WAS CLOSE to nightfall by the time he left Davis and hit the road that took him north. He phoned Kinsolving from a highway cafe.

"I'm on my way back," Joseph told him. "Things are starting to piece themselves together. But I need to speak with Tippett..."

"I told you, he's gone missing..."

"Then I need to speak with his roommate what's his name again?"

"Roper. Steven Roper." Kinsolving hesitated. "But I promised I wouldn't divulge their address..."

"Who'd you promise?"

"Tippett."

"Then give me Roper's address."

"But they live together."

"I thought you said Tippett is missing..."

"Yes."

"Then they don't live together, do they?"

In the end, he managed to construct the linguistic rational so Kinsolving could give him the information he needed without feeling he might be struck down by a lightning bolt for betraying a sacred trust. It was that power of language, which made a mockery of standard notions of truth and falsehood, allowing both politicians and journalists to survive and enabling both to take advantage of priests like Kinsolving.

Chapter 53

ROPER'S PLACE WAS in a dingy block of flats stuck out near the railroad yards, in the old industrial section of Capital City. Joseph took out the slip of paper on which he written the address and apartment number Kinsolving had given him.

It was the kind of place they kept society's throwaways, Joseph thought, looking up at the grimy woodframe building. For dopers and alcoholics and people on the run.

The hallway had a tenement house smell of cheap food and ninety-nine cent wine. He walked up the creaking steps and wondered how much time they had left before they caved in.

Apartment number six was on the second floor. He knocked and waited. Then he heard a voice ask who it was.

"Telegram!" he answered.

The door opened. A slim young man with a pretty face and a wispy blond moustache opened the door and looked at Joseph suspiciously. "Who's it for?" he asked.

"Miles Tippett," Joseph said, looking at the blond and thinking he was just a kid. He reached into his jacket and took out an envelope and waved it in his face.

"Miles isn't here," said the kid. "I'll take it..."

Joseph shook his head. "Sorry," he said. "Company regulations. Maybe you can tell me where he is?"

The kid looked annoyed. "I don't know where he is. But I'm his roommate. you can just leave it with me. Or else I'll have him call..."

"Suit yourself," said Joseph, sticking the envelope back in his pocket. "But you might tell him its a lot of money and he'll have to go to Redding to collect it."

"How do you know it's money?" asked the kid.

"Because I had to sign for it," said Joseph, turning around and starting to walk toward the stairs.

"Wait a second!" said the kid.

Joseph looked back.

The kid had his lips tightly pursed, as if he was trying to think of something fast. "Hold on," he said, retreating into the apartment and closing the door behind him.

Going over to the apartment door, Joseph put his ear against the wood. He thought he could make out some whispered conversation but not the words.

After a minute or so, the door opened again. The blond kid smiled out at him. "Listen, couldn't I just sign for it? I can show you identification..."

"Sorry," said Joseph. "No can do."

The smile faded from blondy's lips. Joseph could almost hear his small mind working, trying to figure something out. He wasn't too bright, Joseph thought. If this kid was a linguist, then the Marsden Institute was in trouble.

"Look," said Joseph, giving him a little wink. "I'd like to help you out. Do you have a phone?"

"A phone?" The kid pulled on one of his wispy blond whiskers. "Who do you want to call?"

"My boss," said Joseph, pushing his way past.

The kid hadn't been expecting that. He just stood at the door and gawked, following Joseph with his eyes, as he waltzed his way in.

It was a small place. The living room was like a hat box for someone with a tiny head. Six suitcases took up half the area.

"Going somewhere?" Joseph asked.

"Yeah," said the kid, still staring at Joseph like a boy with hay sticking out of his ears who'd just seen a pea disappear under a nut shell for the first time in his life.

"Lot of luggage," said Joseph, pointing to the suitcases. "Are both of you leaving or is Tippett going by himself?"

"I told you, Miles isn't here..." he said, looking nervously over Joseph's shoulder.

"Strange," said Joseph, turning toward a door that led off to another room behind him. "I thought I heard voices."

"TV," said the kid, whose cheeks had turned red. "Look, I thought you were going to make a telephone call.."

"Maybe I should turn it off for you." Joseph took a few steps toward the inner door. "You don't want too many alpha waves polluting the air..."

"Hey! Stay out of there!" the kid shouted.

But before Joseph could touch the handle, the door opened on its own. A figure stood in the passageway skinny, small, with a face full of craters probably cause from scratching zits.

"I...I'm sorry, Miles," the kid babbled. "This guy just pushed his way in..."

"That's alright," Tippett said, "don't worry about it..."

"He says he has some money for you..."

"Why don't you go take a walk, Roper," said Joseph, turning toward the kid. "Pick up a lollypop or something. Tippett and I got some talking to do."

The kid stared at Tippett as if waiting for instructions.

"Go ahead," said Tippett. "Do as he says. Come back in about half an hour. By then we'll be through..."

Chapter 54

"HE DOESN'T KNOW anything," said Tippett after the kid had gone. "He just thinks we're running off together. For him it's a great adventure." Tippett smiled to himself and shook his head. "It's so sweet to be young..."

"It's not so sweet if your nice young body starts drying up in the slammer," said Joseph, taking out his cigarettes and offering him one.

A tear trickled down Tippett's pockmarked face. He

189

stared at Joseph like a mangy dog without anything to say.

"Why don't you tell me what happened," Joseph prompted. "It all started in Guatemala, didn't it?"

Tippett nodded. "In a small Mayan village, deep in the highlands. It was where the New World Church had set up its base. Several of us from the Marsden Foundation were assigned to them as translators. The new government gave us pretty much anything we wanted. It was a great place to be for a while..."

"What kind of stuff were you doing there?" asked Joseph.

"Basic missionary work. We started a school and a church. We brought in a fair number of converts. But there was a small group that held out. Then there was talk of some Indians who pretended to be Christians but kept to their own secret rituals. With the help of the military, Cross set up a system of informants. Special rations were given to people who provided information. The better the information, the more you got. Since the military had taken most of their land away from them, some of the Indians were close to starvation. So an information network wasn't hard to start. But Cross was never able to get his hands on the real prize..."

"Who was that?"

"The daykeeper. He's the high priest of the Mayas. The one who can interpret the prophecies for them. One day, though, we found this young Indian who had a grudge against him for some reason I don't know what. Cross took the kid in and worked on him for a week. By the time he was done, the young man – his name was Ramirez – was willing to do anything for Cross."

"What did Cross ask him to do?"

"To keep an eye open for signs of what Cross told him was devil worship. But unleashing those kind of passions is dangerous – you never know where it's going to lead..."

Joseph took in a lung full of smoke and thought that he had some experience with passions leading to unknown destinations, himself. "But this time it lead to the daykeeper, I take it?"

"Yes. Ramirez was able to follow the daykeeper to his cache where he kept his ritual artefacts."

"And he told Cross?"

"He was going to tell Cross. But I happened to be at the mission when he came in, all excited. He blurted it out to me..."

"And what did you do?" asked Joseph.

"By that time I was already questioning what Cross was up to. I'd become friendly with an archaeologist who had set up camp near there. I knew that Cross had it in mind to destroy any artefact that was used in a ceremonial way he thought they were all sent by the devil. So I told Professor Stanton about the find..."

"Professor Stanton? He was the archaeologist who was stationed there?"

"Yes. Do you know him?" Tippett asked.

"Only by reputation," Joseph muttered. "Go on..."

"Stanton, of course, was incredibly excited when I told him. But what thrilled him even more was when he heard about the codex..."

"The codex?" Joseph asked. "Was there a hieroglyphic codex there?"

"Not in the cache. But when I took Ramirez to meet Stanton, he told about seeing the daykeeper chanting from a hieroglyphic book at his secret retreat. Stanton told Ramirez that if he could get that book, it would be worth a lot of money to him..."

"He actually said that?"

"In so many words, yes. Ramirez, though, said it would be difficult. He didn't know where the codex was kept."

"But the other stuff, in the cave..."

"Stanton started making an inventory. But Cross found out and used his influence to get him deported."

"Did anyone know about your involvement?" asked Joseph

"No," Tippett said. "Stanton realized my position. Everything was on the hush..."

"Except Ramirez."

"Yes. But Ramirez had gold fever by then or so I found out. After Stanton left, I had forgotten about the codex. For all I knew, it was just in the Indian's imagination. Besides, the chances that it was a legitimate find was pretty slim."

"About as rare as snarks in Mongolia, I suspect," said Joseph. "Only three in the world, I understand."

"Then, one night some months later, there was a knock at the door of my hut. I opened it to find Ramirez, standing there glassyeyed, holding a burlap sack. I brought him inside. He opened the sack and showed it to me. I quickly inspected it. By that time I had studied enough ancient Mayan texts to know what it was. But I certainly didn't have the skills to determine whether it was a forgery. Ramirez, of course, wanted to know how much it was worth. I said I couldn't be certain. I asked him how much he wanted. He said, five hundred dollars..."

"Five hundred?" Joseph said with surprise.

"But who knew whether it was genuine?" said Tippett. "I had no idea what it was worth. And anyway, five hundred was a fortune to Ramirez. I think he reached for the first number that came into his mind."

"So what did you settle on?" asked Joseph.

"I had two hundred dollars in my wallet. I gave him half. He seemed satisfied with that..."

"So you gave him a hundred dollars?"

"Yes." Tippett's expression grew somber. "It was only after he left and I inspected the codex again, that I saw the stains. I rubbed my finger over it and found it still wet..."

"You meant the ink?"

"No, the paper. It was covered in blood."

Joseph felt himself cringe, even though he knew that was where the story was headed. "How did you smuggle it out of the country?"

"It wasn't hard. The New World people had a special relationship with the government, as I said. When we left, our bags weren't touched."

"How about US customs?"

"I've been through it before. I knew they'd give me just a cursory look. Even if they saw, it would have meant nothing to them. It only means something if you know what you're looking for."

"And after you got back?"

"I went to see Stanton at the university. When he saw what I brought him, he nearly had a heart attack. He immediately called in a colleague someone who was an expert in dating..."

"Felix Manning, right?"

"Yes."

"And what did they tell you?"

"That they'd have to run a lot of tests. But no matter what, even if it was fake, they wanted to buy it for the university museum."

"How much did they offer?"

"Five hundred dollars."

"Just what Ramirez said. Maybe he's a better appraiser than you thought."

"Maybe," said Tippett.

"And you sold it to them for five hundred bucks?"

"I just wanted my investment back. As far as I was concerned, I saved it from being destroyed by Cross..."

"How about the daykeeper?" Joseph asked.

Tippett was quiet for a moment. "I don't know what happened to him..."

Joseph stubbed out his cigarette in a paper cup that was sitting on the table next to him and lit another one up. "So, I guess you figured that was that until you saw Ramirez again."

"We met just by chance a few years back," said Tippett. "He was one of the migrants at the labor camp. I just happened to pass him in the street one day. I didn't recognize him, but he recognized me. he followed me and when he found the time was right, he came up and made his demands..."

"He had found out the codex was worth a lot of money, I suppose..."

"Yes. And by that time, I had found out myself. You must have read about it in the newspapers..."

Joseph shrugged. "I usually pass up the art news, myself..."

"It got quite a play. The press said that if it was proved to be an original, it would be worth over a million dollars..."

"I guess that came as quite a blow to you," said Joseph.

"Not really." He said it in such a way that Joseph nearly believed him.

"What did you do when Ramirez made his demand?"

"I told him I didn't have any money. I told him how much I sold the codex for and that I'd give him half – I figured he deserved it. But he wanted more..."

"So you went back to Stanton?"

"No. By that time I knew the codex had been purchased by an art conglomerate and that the person who was the head of that conglomerate was here..."

"Who was that?" asked Joseph.

"A man named Adler. He has a big vacation house in Ecstasy, overlooking the river..."

"Yes," grunted Joseph. "I know the place. You set up a meeting with him?"

"I was scared. But what else could I do?" asked Tippett.

"And what did he say?"

"He told me not to worry. That he'd take care of it. A few days later, Sheriff Larson came to see me. We drove up to the labor camp and waited in his car. He asked me to point out Ramirez to him. We waited about an hour till Ramirez appeared back at the camp and I could finger him..."

"What did Larson do then? Arrest him?"

"No. He just drove away..."

"And the next day Ramirez just happened to be found

dead in the strawberry field," said Joseph.

Tippett's face had turned ashen. "A few days later, yes. But I never thought..." His voice trailed off.

"That wasn't the end, though, was it?"

Tippett slowly shook his head.

"Somehow Cross found out about the codex, didn't he? He knew Ramirez. So he must have put two and two together and probably thought the codex came from the cave..."

"Yes," said Tippett. "He was furious."

"So he decided to create another codex – a forged one. After all, he had access to the ancient paper. And he had the artisans..."

Tippett nodded.

"You told Adler, didn't you?"

Tippett nodded again.

"And that's when Felix Manning came to town. He took over the Gazette. But that was a front, wasn't it? His real purpose was to sabotage Cross – with your help, of course."

"It wasn't that simple," said Tippett.

"I suppose not," Joseph replied.

"Somehow Cross found out," Tippett said. "My life was in danger. I had to run..."

"And you went to Adler for more money? Wasn't that dangerous?"

"Yes. But I had no alternative," said Tippett. "I didn't know what else to do. I didn't have any money of my own. Anyway, Adler said he'd give me enough to start life someplace else but only after Cross' forgery was exposed."

"So you went to Kinsolving. He helped you find a safe house..."

"I just told him I was running from Cross. That was enough for him."

"But then you called the Gazette a few days ago. Why?"

"I was panicking. I wanted to get away as fast as I could. I wasn't able to get a hold of Manning, so I decided to call the other archaeologist..."

"What other one?"

"The young woman. I had seen her with Manning at the university. Then I saw her again at the Gazette. She took me to see Adler and talked to him on my behalf..."

"When was that?"

"A couple of days ago," he said.

"She took you to Adler's place?"

"Yes."

"Who did you meet with?"

"Adler."

"Just Adler? Was he the only one there?"

"I just met with him. But there were others. I could hear voices in the other room," he said.

"Anyone you recognized?"

"I don't know. It was pretty muffled. But once Adler left the room. I picked up the phone to call Steven and someone was on the line..."

"Did you hear what they were saying?"

"Not much. They were arranging for a collection of something..."

"From Adler's house?"

"Yes, I think so."

"Do you know what was going to be collected?"

"No. That's all I heard. Then I put down the phone."

Joseph stared at him hard. "How do you feel about all this?"

"Like shit!"

"You might feel like shit," said Joseph, "but Salvador Garcia probably feels worse."

"Don't you think I realize that?" he said. "I haven't slept through the night for the last two years."

"Well, maybe I can help you get a few good winks," said Joseph taking a pen and paper out of his pocket. "Start writing!" he ordered.

"What'll I say?" asked Tippett, looking at him helplessly.

"Don't worry, I'll dictate it to you."

Chapter 55

HE CHECKED HIS watch when he left Tippett's place. It was close to midnight. His head was spinning from lack of sleep and his stomach ached for reasons too numerous to mention.

He tried ringing Kinsolving but couldn't find him in.

On the way out of town he passed a motel with flashing neon lights that looked cheap enough for his wallet and plastic enough to keep out the rodents. A few hours sleep was all he needed. A few hours sleep and then everything would come together for him.

Chapter 56

HE WOKE WITH a start. The sun was beating in through the curtainless window. He sprinkled some water over his face and threw his clothes back on. He should have felt better, seeing that he had a signed statement from Tippett which he figured, if Beekman wasn't a total fraud, would be enough to buy Salvador's ticket to freedom. But he left the dingy motel feeling worse than the night before when he had dumped himself there.

What was playing on him like a rotary drill in his brain, what had finally sunk in, what he now knew without qualification was that he had been played for a sucker. He'd been used like a pawn in an intricate game of chess – or a snot rag. And neither idea made him feel any better than yesterday's supper.

But all the pieces of the puzzle weren't totally played out.

And the continuing ache in his stomach seemed to be a prelude for trouble yet to come.

It was a quick drive to Ecstasy. The moist woodlands were beckoning. But the allure for him was over if it ever had been there at all. He could have just as easily been driving to a camp for the criminally insane rather than a fishing resort, as far as he was concerned.

As he came into town, he saw a dark cloud hovering. It was as if someone had rewound a bad film and played it back to him. Just like the first time he had arrived, a strong, acrid odor shot up his nostrils and his eyes were almost blinded by the pollutants that hung heavy in the air.

He made his way down Second Street and parked across from what was left of the Gazette. This time there weren't any fire engines. The place had just been left to burn itself down.

He got out and leaned against the fender of his car, staring across at the steaming ruins.

The biggest of the Panchos was standing by the remains. His large frame stooped, kicking at a smouldering cinder. Joseph walked over to him. Pancho turned and his massive face, so hard and ugly before, seemed softened by a kind of macho grief, like a bull that had its tail lopped off by an angry matador.

"This town go loco, senior," he said, shaking his head. "In Mexico there is one night when El Diablo escapes from the grave and does bad things. But never nothing like this..."

"What happened, Pancho?" he asked.

"Gringos with guns. First they come here, then they go to the labor camp. They ask, 'Where is the Indians?' But there ain't no Indians – all of them, they left. So the gringos, they get more angry. They get into their trucks and head for the Indian barrio over there..." He pointed west, to the other side of the river.

"You mean the commune?" asked Joseph. "The one the missionaries set up?"

Pancho nodded. "Si, senior. That place..."

"But why?" asked Joseph.

"They say the Indians have killed some ninos and used them for their sacrifices. But me, I think that when gringos get angry, they want to kill Indians. And where else are there Indians, senior?"

"But the state police," said Joseph. "They didn't just let it happen, did they?"

"Sure, they come. But they come too late. The village, it was already burned down..."

"What happened to the people?"

"Some of them, maybe they are burned in their adobes. The rest, they share a cave with los coyotes now..."

Joseph stared at him in silence.

The big man reached into a pocket of his dungarees. "Your woman friend, before she go, she ask me to give you this." He handed Joseph an envelope.

Joseph took it and stared over at the ruins. Somewhere, under the charred embers, was the press that beautiful instrument of destruction. The waves led from there across the river to the Indian village in one night's orgy of violence.

"When did she leave?" he asked.

"Yesterday, senior. On her stupid bicycle. She was in much of a hurry."

"Which way did she go?" asked Joseph.

The big man pointed in the direction of a lonely house on a hill overlooking the horizon.

Chapter 57

SPEEDING AROUND CURVES at sixty on the clock and gearing down for maximum power, spraying dirt behind him and barely keeping the tires on the road, he headed for a house that had been pointed out to him before. One that had stayed in his mind.

It was pink and grand, sitting on the hill top and looming over the river like a castle of a California nobleman.

When he got to the top of the hill, he headed directly for the gate, mashing on his brakes and screeching to a halt with just inches to spare between the steel bars and the grid of his front end.

A few seconds more and he might have made it. But he was just moments too late.

He saw the helicopter, its propeller blade whipping up the air, on a patch of land at the far end of the estate. Three figures were running toward it – a man with greying hair, who, even from a distance exuded wealth like an elderly, well-dressed peacock; a taller man, dressed in a white suit whose silhouette Joseph had known before; and a young woman dressed in black, wearing a straw hat and clutching it tightly against the whirling force of the wind.

The woman and the man dressed in white were hand in hand. The three bundled into the copter and then it took off.

Joseph felt the blast of hot air in his face.

Gazing through the bars, on the other side of the gate, he saw a black Honda Civic. Learning against it was Gabriella's bicycle.

He watched the whirlybird fly off into the distance headed for the nearest international airport, he bet and then, reaching into his pocket, he took out the envelope that Pancho had given him. He read it through, quickly:

"I wish it could have happened some other way," she wrote. "But there's important work to be done to save a glorious civilization from ruins and not much time remains. I hope you can forgive me..." Underneath she had scribbled her initials, "G.L."

"At least she was honest about something," he muttered to himself, looking at the initials and realizing that it cut both ways. Then, crumpling the paper, he let it drop to the ground.

Chapter 58

HE DROVE BACK through the ravaged town, past the smouldering ruins of the sausage plant and the Gazette and out onto the highway. Turning on the radio, he fiddled with the dial. The airwaves were full of bad vibrations:

"We're getting reports from up and down the coast, but it's hard to separate rumor from fact ... people here are still massed in the streets ... neighborhoods have been sealed off by police ... the smell of gas is everywhere ... all bridges into San Francisco have been closed ... no one's certain yet of the death toll in the double decker freeway collapse..."

Maybe this was it, he thought. Maybe this was California's own Armageddon.

For the first time he hoped that Polly had actually done what she had threatened – taken the kids and flown off to her parents.

He stopped at a service station to use the phone. He tried dialing his number at home but all he got was a recording saying for him to try again later since the lines were overloaded.

He phoned the refuge and asked for Kinsolving.

"I blame myself," said Kinsolving, when he got on the phone. "I knew that town was a tinder box. I don't think we truly understood the amount of resentment the people in town had against the commune..."

"But why did a story about forged artefacts cause them to go crazy like that?"

"It wasn't the artefacts," said Kinsolving. "They couldn't have cared less about that. It was the strawberries..."

"The strawberries?"

"Over the last few years, the strawberry farms around here have been going bankrupt. The wholesalers, it seems, had decided their fruit was substandard. They were getting bigger and better strawberries from someplace else. But the origin of this new supply was a mystery to the farmers until yesterday, I guess."

Suddenly, Joseph understood. "So it was that little piece Gabriella wrote about the giant strawberries the commune was growing?"

"It was a deep medieval hatred that had been suddenly released – like a feudal mob that goes after the manor when their harvest fails..."

"Except these guys took it out on the servants, not the Count," Joseph pointed out. "On the other hand, nobody in this country has ever been sent up river for killing Indians. Unless they were Indians themselves." He thought a minute. "At least that explains why the sausage company was burned down..."

"Why?" asked Kinsolving.

"Because that's where the New World strawberries were being warehoused."

"Maybe something good will come out of it," Kinsolving suggested, as if his profession demanded a silver lining.

"I just heard there was an earthquake in San Francisco. You think something good will come out of that, too?"

"An earthquake in San Francisco? Today? Just now?"

Suddenly Joseph heard the ringing of another phone.

"Hold on a minute," said Kinsolving.

A moment later, Kinsolving was back on the line. "I'm wanted at San Carlos Prison," he said. "An emergency. It's not clear what..."

Chapter 59

GETTING BACK INTO his car, he again drove onto the highway and, in a few minutes, took the turning toward the prison. Thinking it over, he felt it was a final gesture, before he left to face his own ruins back in Frisco. If nothing else, he could deliver the statement that Tippett had written. Then he would be done. And, as Kinsolving might have said, from the ashes of the carnage one good thing could come.

Driving east through the countryside, it wasn't long before the massive institution appeared, looming below the foothills. He continued down the access road, the way he had gone once before, and focused on the glowering structure as it got progressively larger.

Then a curious thing happened. Perhaps it was just in his mind, but the closer he came to the prison gates, the slower he seemed to go. Suddenly, the atmosphere had become heavy and dense, like he had hit an invisible barrier. It felt as if he were driving into a cosmic bubble.

Behind him, the huge crimson sun was slowly dropping in the western sky, filling the horizon and causing an enormous shadow to grow from the front of his car, casting a pall of darkness before him.

He parked by the side of the road, got out and began walking toward the grassy area by the prison gates, as if he were wearing shoes of lead.

It struck him immediately as he began to walk. Perhaps it was an instinctive understanding that something was wrong, something he couldn't define in rational terms but, nonetheless, still felt.

He slowly looked around, trying to piece together the images that entered his mind and finally began to realize what had first hit his subconscious. He noticed that the massive encampment of Indians which he had seen before, was beginning to break up. Tepees were being taken down, tents were being rolled and tied. Yet everything was being done so quietly that it was hard to see a great movement had begun.

He came up alongside an old man with an ancient face chiselled by the sands of time who was staring out at the prison walls. He stood by the man, silently, gazing out in the

203

same direction, trying to see what he was staring at.

The old man turned to look at him and Joseph could see the light in his eyes. The man made a movement with his hand, a delicate movement of flight.

"I saw it," he sad. "A great white bird. It was perched on the wall. And then it flew off..." The old man pointed his brown, wrinkled finger toward the south.

As Joseph turned to look, he saw something else. What he saw was a familiar figure underneath a maple tree, or perhaps it was an oak, kneeling down as if in prayer.

Joseph walked over to Kinsolving and stood next to him. Neither of them spoke.

He waited there silently for a while until Kinsolving stood up and softly said, "He's dead, Joseph..."

"I know," Joseph replied.

"Somehow he got hold of a knife. He cut into his chest and tried to pull his own heart out..."

"When did it happen?" asked Joseph.

"Several hours ago...I don't know...they wouldn't say. If he could only have held out until I saw him. We were so close, so very close..." The sound of his words drifted off.

Joseph stared out at the retreating shadow. "The gods were angry," he said. "Maybe now they're not..."

Chapter 60

THERE SEEMED TO be a calmness in the air, as there often is after a devastating storm that leaves, along with a trail of destruction, a sense of peace – the serenity of a great force expended; like the quiet and ghostly beauty in the wake of a nuclear bomb.

Stopping at a roadside cafe, he tried to make a call. The telephone lines to San Francisco were still jammed up. He imagined half of them buried under a pile of rubble, left over from the quake, ringing forlornly, but buried so deep that no one could hear them.

He had some coffee and then tried again, later. This time, surprisingly, he got through. He heard his answering machine click on. But there was only one message that was parrotted back to him:

"Joseph? I'd like to see you once more before I go. Meet me tonight at the spot we met – not the last time, but the one before. Do you remember? I'll be there at ten o'clock. I'll wait a half hour. I don't know whether or not you'll get this message in time, but if you do, please try to come. There's something I need to say and I can only say it to you in person..."

Chapter 61

IT WAS ALMOST ten at night when he reached the campus community across the bay from San Francisco. Driving along the marina, he could see the skyline of the city to the south was still gleaming brightly. In fact, as he turned off the highway, toward Berkeley, there was hardly any sign of physical damage at all. Yet the aura of the quake still hovered in the air, he thought. He felt it in the neighborhoods he passed through; he saw it in the eyes of the people who filled the streets like refugees from some unexplained event which had thrown them all into another world – a different universe where even the most mundane fact could no longer be taken for granted.

The cafes were crowded, he noticed as he parked his car not far from the central campus. But they weren't buzzing like they normally would. Rather, people sat around in wondrous silence communicating without words an awesome communality.

The campus, however, the green and the meadow, was deserted. On an ordinary evening, he thought, there would have been the occasional lovers, strolling hand in hand, or at least a stray dog. But now, it seemed, people preferred to cling together in knots, as if needing the warmth of a cluster.

He walked alone into the darkness, with only the moonlight and his memory to guide him till he came to a little grove by a bubbling brook. And he remembered that night, so long ago now, when they had met to say goodbye, only to come together again in another life.

Then he noticed her sitting on a wooden bench, nestled under a copse of eucalyptus – the soft ivory of the lamplight shrouding her hair. She turned and he could see the magnificently green luminescence of her eyes.

She saw him and smiled. "I was hoping you'd come," she said.

He walked over to her bench and sat down beside her. Gazing out at the brook, reflecting the mixture of moonglow and radiant electricity, he said, "Does Hannah know?"

"Hannah's image of me rests in scrap books," she said. "I could never compete with that. As far as she's concerned, it's better to let her believe that I evaporated in the fire..."

He looked at her face. She was gazing into the darkness, without bitterness or malice, he thought. Just gazing into the mystery of night.

"When you called me from the Zuni you had already broken up with Felix, hadn't you..."

"Yes," she said. "We had gone our separate way for some time. But we still had to settle our affairs."

"His scheme to make a fortune on antiquities futures – you weren't a part of that?"

"Just in so far as I understood what he was attempting to do and decided not to stand in his way." She gazed at him in a dreamy manner in a way he remembered from so long ago. "The idea of reinventing myself, of starting a new life, appealed to me..."

206

"It always did," he said.

"Don't you remember the way it was, Joseph? When the world was still fresh?" Her eyes sparkled with girlish enthusiasm. "There was so much to do and we were going to do it all, weren't we?"

"You were, at least," he replied.

"But it's all still possible!" she said, taking his hand. "You just have to grab for a star, Joseph, and pull it down from the sky..."

"As long as you don't fry your fingers in the process."

She shook her head. "Poor, sweet Joseph," she said. "Always afraid of burning your fingers..."

"Or someone else's. You heard what happened to Salvador Garcia, I expect..."

"Yes," she said, her expression suddenly changing like the twin faces of drama, he thought. One happy, the other sad. "We were so close, weren't we? I found Gonzalez the farm worker who had run away in Mexico. I got a statement from him saying Ramirez was blackmailing Tippett and that he had told Gonzalez he was frightened for his life the day before he was killed. He knew Salvador had been set up. We had it all on video tape. I'm sure the appeals court would have accepted that..."

"How long had you been working with Beekman?" Joseph asked.

"Just a month or so," she replied. "It was part of my agreement with Felix. He needed the New World group exposed. I needed Salvador..."

"You always needed people like Salvador," he said. "They were such a good focus for your guilt. Otherwise you'd have to waste it on things like too many plastic bottles in the trash..." He rubbed the side of his aching head. "I suppose it wasn't too difficult getting the bodies from the anatomy lab. It was just a matter of getting the fire hot enough to gassify the flesh. How did you manage that?"

"I left that to Felix and his young lady..."

"You preferred playing Dash, I guess. Beekman's gumshoe."

"It suits me, don't you thank?" she asked, smiling again.

"One thing does puzzle me," he said. "How were you going to collect? I mean the insurance money all went to the Institute in Belize. Felix, Stanton and their charming young partner can take advantage of that. But how about yourself?"

"I was given shares in antiquities futures..."

"So everybody wins," he said. "Adler has a genuine codex for his collection and the commodity market in antiquities soars, turning a million dollars into a hundred million, I suppose. Felix, Stanton and Gabriella or should I say Genevieve? have a well-endowed institute even if they have to run it with phoney names. But, as you said, it can be sort of nice to reinvent yourself, can't it? Especially if you can reinvent yourself rich..."

"And the baddies lost," she said. "Like Mundt and Cross and Grimes..."

"And Salvador and Kinsolving and all the missionary Indians?" he asked.

"I'm not responsible for that," she said.

"I guess not," he replied. And then, looking out into the night, he asked, "Are you staying with Beekman?"

"Beekman?" she laughed. "He was only a means to an end."

"Like me?"

She lowered her head onto his shoulder and he could smell the perfume of her hair. "Not like you, Joseph. We're friends..."

He turned to look at her and she kissed him on the mouth.

"What's that line again?" he asked. "Oh, yes. 'My lips have tasted bitter fruit...'"

"I don't understand," she said.

"A line from a poem Hannah showed me," he replied.

"Oh..."

They sat in silence for a while and then she took his hand

again and caressed it. "Joseph," she whispered. "Come away with me. I have enough money for us to do what we always wanted. We could start a newspaper together someplace far away. The world is ours, Joseph..."

"Radkin and Dash," he said. "Sounds too much like a one hour laundry."

"We can change our names," she said.

"To what?"

"Whatever we want."

He was quiet for a bit and then he said, "I sort of feel comfortable with my name. It's like an old hat, you know. It might be frayed and out-of-style, but, somehow, you don't want to give it up..."

She turned and kissed him on the nose and smiled, sympathetically. "You're the same old Joseph, aren't you? You'll never change."

"I guess not," he said.

She stood up. "That's why we could never make it before. You were never able to reach out for the stars, were you?"

"Sometimes I reach out," he said. "Everybody does. But the stars are up there for the world, Elizabeth. Not just those special people with wonderful eyes and silken hair..."

"That's why you got on so well with my mother," she replied, taking a few steps toward the rushing brook and ten turning back around.

"Hannah's a wonderful woman," said Joseph.

"And she deserves a son like you, not a daughter like me," she said.

"What she deserves is to know that you're alive," he said. "She loves you very much..."

"But you won't say anything about me being alive, will you?" Her face was ghostly, bathed in the soft light.

"How do you know I won't say much more than that?" he asked.

"Because you're someone to be trusted," she said.

Chapter 62

THE BRIDGE FROM Berkeley to San Francisco was shut. One of the spans had collapsed – something they said couldn't happen. But they were always saying things couldn't happen, he thought. So when it did, they had to say, "It couldn't happen, but..."

He had to drive down the east side of the bay, all the way to Redwood City and then across, coming back up the peninsula from the south. By the time he reached his house, it was close to midnight.

Parking the car across the street, he got out. And then he saw her, sitting on the steps, underneath the porch light. He walked over and sat next to her.

"I was so worried, Joseph," she said. "When I heard about the earthquake I tried to call..."

"The lines were down for a while," he said.

"I know. I took the first plane back, but it was ages before they let us land..."

She looked at him and he could see that she had been crying. Her eyes were red and her cheeks were stained with tracks of salt. She must have really been upset, he thought. Polly didn't cry easily.

"I had an image of the house collapsed with you under it," she said.

He put his arm around her.

"The only thing I wanted was to be with you, Joseph."

"Even underneath the rubble?"

"Not underneath the rubble. Like we were. Like we used to be..."

"We can never be like we used to be," he replied.

"Don't you want to try and make it work?" she asked.

"Yes. But we can never be like we used to be. No one can."

She buried her head in his chest and began to weep. And he petted her hair and said, "I love you, Polly."

"I love you, too, Joseph," she said, between sobs. "But why won't you try?"

"I do try," he said. "But in the end, I can't help being myself..."

Chapter 63

IT WAS TWO in the morning, after he had woken the children and given them their hugs and told them that he was glad they were safely home again. They had wanted a story, so he had told them the one he had told them many times before, about a mischievous monkey who had gotten lost from the zoo and was kept hidden underneath their beds. And then he tucked them in as Polly watched.

When Polly had fallen asleep in his arms, cuddled up on the couch, he had slipped away to his desk.

He rolled a piece of paper into the typewriter, thought a minute and then began:

"This is a story about time. Not the time that passes like the ticking of a clock, but the battle of mythologies that gives time definition.

"It's a story about people who thought they could travel in time, slipping back and forth between future and past using only their imaginative abilities of recreation.

"But this story is also about power and the lust for wealth. It's about greed and hatred and even cold-blooded murder. It's about stolen promises and betrayal of trusts. In short, it's about our brave new world, the world we've created, all of us.

"And it starts with the haunting face of a young Mayan Indian..."

Suddenly, he felt her presence behind him.

211

"It's good to see you hard at work," she whispered in his ear. Then, glancing over the copy, she asked, "Have you started writing science fiction?"

"No," he said, "it's an article about financial shenanigans concerning Central American antiquities."

She was silent at first. Then she said, "I guess it's only a first draft."

It was at that moment he knew he was well and truly home again.

www.ingramcontent.com/pod-product-compliance
Lightning Source LLC
Chambersburg PA
CBHW020114180626
46812CB00006B/2590